"Exactly wh_____?"

Misty slipped around Tucker and danced up the first couple of steps of the hotel stairwell. "I just want to experience that dangerous thrill of possibly being caught," she replied invitingly.

Her eyes sparkled as he advanced on her. He stood one step below her and pulled her close, finding himself incredibly aroused as she trembled. Her nipples jutted against the soft weave of her top as he undid the row of tiny buttons.

Now he was the one trembling. "You're playing with fire here," he warned her, "and I know all about fire. How easily it can rage out of control." He drew his hands slowly over her shoulders to her breasts, then spun her around and gripped her hips from behind.

"I could push up that skirt of yours, slide right into you," he murmured in her ear, playing into her fantasy. "Anyone floors above, or below, would hear you scream as you climaxed." She moaned and her breaths began to shorten as his hands worked themselves around her buttocks and then slowly upward to cup her exposed breasts.

Just then the squeal of a metal door opening just above them ripped through the air. They froze. Two men talking, and they were coming down. *Oh, God,* Tucker thought frantically, *looks like this fantasy is about to come true....*

Blaze™

Dear Reader,

I've always been seduced by the idea of a place where people could go and safely indulge in their most private, forbidden fantasies. Fortunately I write for Blaze, where I can create just such a place! Of course, a resort like Blackstone's probably couldn't exist in the real world. (All those pesky laws and things!) But it sure was fun imagining what it might be like if it did.

I hope you enjoy your foray into Sin City as Misty and Tucker discover that, sometimes, the real world is far more interesting than make-believe could ever be.

Happy reading (and fantasizing!),

Donna Kauffman

Books by Donna Kauffman

HARLEQUIN BLAZE
18—HER SECRET THRILL
46—HIS PRIVATE PLEASURE

HARLEQUIN TEMPTATION
828—WALK ON THE WILD SIDE
846—HEAT OF THE NIGHT
874—CARRIED AWAY

AGAINST THE ODDS

Donna Kauffman

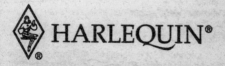

HARLEQUIN®

TORONTO • NEW YORK • LONDON
AMSTERDAM • PARIS • SYDNEY • HAMBURG
STOCKHOLM • ATHENS • TOKYO • MILAN • MADRID
PRAGUE • WARSAW • BUDAPEST • AUCKLAND

This book is dedicated to Vanessa,
who knows all about being up against the odds.
And beating them.
(No woo woo elements, sis!)
Happy Birthday

ISBN 0-373-79073-2

AGAINST THE ODDS

Copyright © 2003 by Donna Jean.

Visit us at www.eHarlequin.com

Printed in U.S.A.

1

SIN CITY.

Tucker Greywolf stepped out of the taxi and paused, intent on absorbing all of it. The bright lights, the steady stream of cars up and down the strip, the excited buzz of the crowd bustling in and out of the endless number of casinos, resorts and clubs.

"First time in Vegas?" the valet asked him, noting his fascination.

Tucker grinned. "That obvious, huh? Yeah, I'm just a small-town boy from New Mexico who lucked out on the location of some seminars I signed up for."

The stooped older man looked up at Tucker's six-plus height, peered into his eyes, then smirked. "Not too small a town, I'm betting." He had a bit of an accent. Russian or Scandinavian. "What convention you here for?"

"No convention," Tucker replied, pulling his wallet out of the back pocket of his jeans to pay the cabbie. "Just some training in forensics the LVMPD has put together."

The valet's bushy white brows lifted. "Forensics? I was right about you then. Small town." He shook his head on a snort, then whistled for a bellman.

"Okay, so Canyon Springs has more than one stop

light, but it's hardly a hotbed of crime. I probably won't ever use this stuff.''

"You a cop in this town of yours?"

"Fire marshal. Just indulging my own professional interest.''

The valet winked at him. "Hopefully you'll indulge in other more personal interests while you're here, no? She's not always a lady, this town." He took the bills Tucker offered him and motioned the bellman to take his bags inside. "But she never fails to show her guests a good time.''

"I bet she does. But I'm really just here for the classes. Might play a hand or two of blackjack or spin the roulette wheel, but—"

The old man chuckled. "She'll seduce you. The reluctant ones are always the first to fall.''

Tucker just laughed. "Maybe next time.''

"Ah, Mr. Small Town, you like your privacy." He nodded at the newspaper Tucker had stuck under his arm. "You should try out the new place, then. Specializes in keeping things all hush-hush, you know? So no one back home will be the wiser, eh?"

Tucker could have told him there was no one back home to hide anything from, but the valet was clearly enjoying his attempts to corrupt his latest Vegas virgin. Far be it from him to deny the old guy his fun. Besides, it seemed like a suitable introduction to the City of Sin.

"Blackstone, he doesn't listen to the County boys," he was saying. "Trying to turn Vegas into some kind of family Disneyland with slots." Despite being almost a foot shorter than Tucker, he leaned in with a nod and a wink. "This Blackstone, he knows the kinds of rides people are really looking for when they come here." His laughter turned to a long wheeze that had Tucker thumping him on the back. "Thanks, thanks," he said when he got his wind back.

"No, thank you," Tucker said, and meant it. He enjoyed people who weren't afraid to be themselves. Colorful, some would say. Characters. That was one of the things he liked best about being from a small town. Everyone had a name—and a personal history—to go with their face. There were no strangers in Canyon Springs. Here, he was all but swallowed up by them.

He followed the bellman to the lobby, glancing again at the newspaper while he waited his turn to check in. He'd actually already read the article on the way in from the airport. Apparently many of the Vegas resorts had spent a considerable amount of revenue trying to expand the focus of their attractions beyond the gamblers and high rollers to the families looking for a place to have a good time.

Lucas Blackstone, on the other hand, had unabashedly created an opulent adult oasis of decadence. A very private resort catering to very private desires, tucked away at the edge of the desert.

"I'm sure he won't lack for takers," Tucker murmured with a slight shake of his head. Mr. Blackstone would probably do very well with his posh playground, but he'd have to do it without Tucker Greywolf.

Tucker preferred to fulfill his fantasies on his

own…and he didn't require any high-priced assistance to do so. He tossed the paper away when it was his turn to step to the desk for registration. For now, his fantasies had more to do with solving the mysteries of cold flesh than delving into the pleasures of the more heated variety.

AMETHYST FORTUNA SMYTHE-DAVIES, aka Misty Fortune, as she was known to her legion of fans, peered through the tinted windows of her limo as it wound its way along the serpentine drive leading to the entrance of Blackstone's. "What in God's name have I bloody gone and done?" she murmured beneath her breath.

Of course, she knew exactly what she'd gone and done. She'd sold her soul, and probably a goodly part of her dignity, for the sake of a few screaming orgasms. It had seemed like such a brilliant idea at the time.

The long black sedan slid to the curb, the engine purring quietly as the driver got out and came around to open her door. Her blue-blooded ancestral lineage notwithstanding, Misty didn't usually indulge in what she termed Spoiled Silver Spooners behavior. Normally, she'd have hopped in a cab. However, Blackstone's prided itself on providing privacy along with pleasure, which included a personal escort from the airport in the manner of a sleek black sedan complete with a quietly efficient chauffeur. Considering that her five-day stay here would cost the lion's share of her biannual royalty check, she figured she'd let them pamper her however they saw fit.

She waited for the driver to open her door, but not wanting to betray how shaky she was, even to him, she politely refused his offer of a hand. Once out of her plush cocoon, her nerves jangled even more. *You're a butterfly emerging from your chrysalis,* she told herself. *A lovely, bold monarch seeking pleasure wherever it may be and claiming it for her own.*

God's balls, but her editor would turn as purple as that prose if she ever wrote anything like that in one of her books. Besides, if her prose had a color at all, it would undoubtedly be a throbbing, molten red. Sometimes the words pulsed through her like that, an oozing lava flow, as if she were channeling them from some secret inner source. Very secret, she thought with a private smirk, as her actual knowledge was somewhat limited. Thank heaven for vivid imaginations. She'd banked an entire career on her rather active one.

Misty pushed a hand through the mess of brown curls that hadn't stood up well to a cross-country flight. Glancing down she noticed her long, slim cotton skirt and sleeveless knit pullover hadn't fared any better. *Oh so glamorous as always, Misty,* she thought with a wry smile. Nothing to do about it now, so she turned toward the sleek, black marble of the walls, the carved archway, the etched-glass entrance, and tried to swallow her trepidation.

She had to, because, as she'd recently been forced to admit, vivid imaginations only went so far. Which was why Misty Fortune, author of a string of red-hot erotic bestsellers, had done what any of her forthright and confident heroines would have done when faced with a similar predicament. "Grabbed the problem by the balls and dealt with it," she muttered with gritted determination.

"I beg your pardon, miss?"

She glanced at the driver, privately amused at her unseemly comment, even as her cheeks pinked a bit. The downside to her fair English complexion. Her skin reflected every emotion. "The marble walls really grab your attention, don't they?" she parried, thinking fast. Unseemly language was fine when she was alone, but never in public. Her accent, one that living close to a decade in New York City had barely muted, grew more pronounced, as it always did in moments of stress. "The whole thing is quite lovely, really," she said, offering a smile.

Charmed, the driver smiled and nodded. "To be certain, miss. I'll get your bags."

Misty nodded, then quietly let out a breath when he turned away. She might not be one to tout the silver spoon that had been lodged in her throat at birth—gads, it had taken twenty long years to yank the bloody thing out and toss it back—but she wasn't above occasionally using the years of painful etiquette classes to which she'd been subjected to smooth over a momentary lapse in decorum. Miss Pottingham would be ever so delighted to know her fervor hadn't been entirely for naught.

Misty smiled to herself. Lapses in decorum indeed. To be expected, she supposed, as she'd become a combination of the button-down British city of her birth…and the raucous American one she'd adopted on her twenty-first birthday. To the outward eye, she was a young woman, ever so evenly mannered, suitably dressed and coiffed and well-schooled in how to handle most any social occasion with quiet dignity and panache. On the inside, however, she was nothing like that.

In her mind's eye, she was a Misty Fortune heroine. Bold, daring; an aggressive wanton who saw the world as a ripening piece of fruit, begging her to sink her teeth into its juicy flesh and savor every last decadent drop.

Lapses in decorum, oh she'd had many. Dozens. Hundreds. Maybe thousands. Yet, all but the most minor had been enacted exclusively in the privacy of her imagination…and carefully recorded with pen and paper for the delight and stimulation of her readers.

Until now.

Now she was going to finally experience for real what she'd only ever allowed her heroines to enjoy. Now she was finally going to move beyond her limited personal experiences and indulge in the type of sexual fantasies most women—herself included—only dreamt about. She'd always counted herself lucky that she'd turned those hot, feverish dreams into an annual income that allowed her to live rather well, even by New York City standards.

But, to be honest, it was a little difficult to demand things of your lover that you weren't quite certain you could do yourself. And exactly how did a person go about requesting such things, really? Her characters always met in wildly interesting, larger than life ways, leading them quickly down a carnal path that would never happen in real life. At least not her real life anyway. Leading her to believe that she needed to project a certain confidence in that area to attract a lover with similar preferences. But for that she needed a little help.

Which was exactly why she'd chosen the Continental Concubine package from the very select and amazingly creative menu provided to her in the sleek Blackstone brochure. Apparently her literary successes had drawn the attention of Mr. Blackstone himself, who'd personally invited her to be one of the resort's first guests. It was an invitation she'd initially politely refused.

But the glossy brochure had lain there, silently daring her, taunting her, beckoning her. And her latest story seemed twice-told. Thrice-told. Her last lover even more so. She needed to do something...

Several glasses of champagne, sipped alone on New Year's Eve, had found her perusing the detailed menu once again. She'd told herself it was simply research. She was merely scanning the brochure in hopes something would spark a new light in her gradually dimming imaginary world.

Which didn't explain why she picked up the phone and actually made a reservation. It had taken another couple of glasses to come up with the rationalization for that. And she still wasn't entirely sure she bought it. But here she was, and dammit, she was going to learn how to be a seductive, confident courtesan, skilled in pleasuring any man...therefore able to demand the same for herself. Even if it killed her. Or worse, completely mortified her.

"You're thirty years old. You can do this," she

murmured. "*Be* the heroine." Not believing a word of it, she nonetheless managed to straighten her shoulders and push through the discreet glassed entrance of Blackstone's. Misty Fortune's Wild Las Vegas Adventure was about to begin.

As THE REST of the class began to stand and disperse, Tucker made several last notes, then finally slapped his notebook shut and rolled his shoulders. The seminar on the latest in bloodstain pattern analysis techniques had been fascinating. So much so that he'd knotted his neck and shoulder muscles concentrating on the instructor's lecture while taking notes as fast as possible.

He glanced at his watch. It was almost five. He stood and collected the course materials and his notebook, thinking he'd catch dinner at one of the hotel restaurants he'd scoped out after checking in the night before, maybe indulge in a little blackjack afterward. He'd brought a small stash of play money to have a little fun with. The rule was that once it was gone, his gambling time was up.

He wasn't much of a risk taker anyway. He had enough of that in his job. His fascination centered on the science of uncovering the truth by tying fact with incontrovertible proof. And the incontrovertible truth about Las Vegas was that the house was always going to come out on top. Sort of took the fun out of playing.

He paused by the lectern, waiting for the detective who'd taught the class to finish speaking to one of the other class members. The young woman finally left and the detective turned to him.

"Good lecture," Tucker told him. "I'm especially intrigued by what you were saying about the new Polaroid lenses. I wondered if you had any sources for follow-up information on that."

Detective Miguez held out his hand. "I'm glad you liked the lecture. What department are you with?"

Tucker shook his hand and grinned. "Little town in New Mexico that will probably never need their fire marshal to understand the use of Polaroid lenses in capturing accurate bloodstain pattern pictures. Or their sheriff for that matter. Did you ever work with a detective by the name of Dylan Jackson?"

Miguez's thick brows rose. "Sure did. So you're from…what's the name of—Canyon something-or-other, right?"

"Right. Canyon Springs."

"I'm sorry." He chuckled. "How is Jackson doing? Sheriff, huh?"

"He's great. Just got married in fact."

Miguez's eyebrows reached new heights. "Jackson? Married? Well, I'll be. I guess going home again was the right thing for him to do then. A shame, he was a good detective."

"He's pretty content and the fine citizens of Canyon Springs sleep better with him on the job."

Miguez nodded, though it was clear he didn't quite understand how anyone could be happier away from the action. "So you're a fire marshal? What got you interested in this avenue of forensics?" He returned

Tucker's grin. "Splatter patterns don't generally survive a fire."

"No, sir, they don't. Generally I focus on more fire-specific investigative techniques, but I find all of it fascinating. Dylan heard about these seminars and passed the brochure on to me." Actually, he'd done it as a joke. He'd been goading Tucker to consider moving to the big city for years. They'd always had a friendly rivalry since their high school football days. Jackson had gone to Vegas fresh out of school, but he'd eventually come back home. Didn't stop him from urging Tucker to leave, however. Tucker usually gave it right back to him, accusing him of being worried that the town wasn't big enough for the both of them. "I figured I'd combine a little vacation with a chance to feed my fascination a little."

Miguez nodded, apparently finding it far easier to understand professional obsession, but then a lot of guys in his line of work probably would. "You bring the wife and kids?"

Tucker shook his head. "Don't have either. I figure I'd find something to do to keep busy, though."

"You think?" Miguez said with a laugh. "Well, if it won't cramp your style, how about we catch some dinner and I can fill you in on some contacts you might be interested in following up. I can also get you some info on some other seminars coming up later this spring."

"That'd be great." Tucker let go of his blackjack plans without a second thought.

Miguez shook his head. "Man, you're just as bad

as the rest of us. You ever think of relocating up here? We can always use another sharpie.''

''What, and let Jackson have all the hero worship? No way,'' he joked. Fact was, he'd thought about it many times, starting from the time he'd decided to shift his focus from climbing the ladder toward fire chief to the investigative side instead. But, for a number of reasons, he'd never done more than think about it.

Miguez gathered his tapes and charts. Tucker stepped in and helped him pile everything into the file boxes he'd wheeled in at the beginning of class this morning.

''I hope you don't mind, but one of the other instructors, Bill Patterson, might hook up with us as well. He's with the Medical Examiner's office, specializes in crime scene post mortems.''

The evening was getting better by the minute. ''I'm signed up for his class on Friday. This will give me a chance to pick his brain before the rest of the class gets a hold of him.''

''I'm sure he won't mind,'' Mig said. ''Shop talk is our life.'' He chuckled. ''What am I talking about. What life?''

Tucker smacked the lights off on the way out, thinking he should take vacations like this more often.

SHE WASN'T CUT OUT for vacations like this. Well, a Misty Fortune heroine might be. But her inner Amethyst Fortuna Smythe-Davies was definitely not. This was why she didn't do book tours. She didn't like being the center of attention. It gave her hives.

So why on earth she thought being the focus of such undivided, extremely personal—intimate even—attention was going to be any different she had no idea.

"Thank you," she told Marta, her personal attendant, as the older woman handed her the small leather binder. She did her level best to sign the guest card with an unwavering hand before handing it back to her.

"Are you sure you'd rather have your meal here in your room?" Marta asked. "I'll be happy to set it up out there by the indoor lagoon where you could listen to the waterfall, perhaps take a dip?"

Misty shook her head, but smiled. She realized she wasn't being the most accommodating guest. "This will be fine." Besides, she didn't think she could take any more stimulation. Even something as benign as the gentle sound of water cascading over rocks would likely be too much at the moment.

"I'll be back to escort you at seven, then."

Misty tried not to shudder in trepidation, but wasn't sure she succeeded. It was to Marta's credit and probably extensive training that she didn't appear to notice. And sigh heavily at the hopeless case she'd been assigned.

She'd already determined she'd see to it Marta was tipped handsomely when this five-day ordeal was over. Or put it in her will if, in fact, she did die of mortification.

Marta left as quietly as she'd come and Misty fell heavily back on her bed. Her first day at Blackstone's had been spent in a sort of sensory saturation zone. Who knew a person could actually overdose on sensual stimulation? And she hadn't even done anything sexual yet. Yet. She quivered again.

This preliminary relaxation method had all been explained to her the night before, but she'd been too fatigued from the travel and the nerves to do more than nod and try to quell the panic that had threatened to rise every other minute. The registration process had been discreet, handled in a small, well-appointed lounge by the woman who was to be her personal director for the duration of her stay. If she had any problems, questions or concerns, she was to buzz Janece right away. At any time of the day or night. All of her other needs and requests were to be directed to Marta. Again, 24-7.

She wondered what a Blackstone employee got for working twenty-four hour shifts. Maybe they lived on site. "That'd be interesting," she murmured, smiling. She was also impressed with the high level of organization that went into planning each guest's stay. Other than the various Blackstone personnel she'd dealt with, she'd yet to see one other guest. It was as if this entire, decadent desert oasis was hers alone to enjoy, which she assumed was precisely how Blackstone's intended she feel.

She rolled her head toward the terrace door that led to her private lagoon and briefly entertained taking Marta's suggestion to dine al fresco after all. But that would mean moving. And for all that her nerves still buzzed along inside her, the rest of her was limp with pleasure from the expert ministrations of the most excellent Blackstone staff.

She gazed up at the batik ceiling and thought about

crawling back between the silk sheets and hiding from the remainder of the day's agenda. Her room was an amazing cocoon of silks and pillows, inviting her to climb in and sleep for say, the winter. But that was all part of their expert plan. None of the sessions she'd signed on for would take place here. This was her lair, her private retreat, an intrinsic part of their plan to seduce her into feeling completely at ease.

Her Blackstone experience had begun in this very bed last night. Her bags had been stowed, her clothes neatly hung and put away by the time she arrived in her room. Marta had run a bath for her, layering the water with a special blend of scented oils that had her relaxing despite her nerves. She'd left her to bathe alone—something Misty hadn't thought twice about at the time—with a gentle suggestion that for the best night sleep, the silk sheets on the bed should caress bare skin only.

She'd slept in the buff before, but it had felt a bit strange—if admittedly stimulating—to do so at another's bidding. And she had slept well. Which was a good thing, because she'd risen to find a ribbon-tied scroll slipped beneath her door, instructing her to shower and dress in the silk wrapper hanging on the back of the bathroom door. This was the last thing she'd do for herself all day.

She'd emerged to find a breakfast of fruit, croissants and tea waiting for her on the low patio table by the lagoon. Listening to the gentle waterfall and the birdsong that seemed to emanate from the thick foliage above, she'd sipped her tea and finally relaxed, thinking that she could get used to this kind of pampering. By the time Marta came to collect her for the first of the day's appointments, she'd almost forgotten why she'd really come here.

She managed to cling to her I'm-just-at-a-spa illusions for most of the day. She'd had a full-body mask and peel, followed by a steam, a light lunch, then a manicure and pedicure while receiving a facial. She'd been washed and conditioned, exfoliated and creamed. By the time Marta had led her back to her room, she felt like she was floating, her entire body glowing. And likely it was.

Which was exactly the plan. Because after dinner she was to accompany Marta to where the first phase of her education was to begin. On a massage table. Where every inch of her skin—every inch—was to be well oiled and scented in preparation for her first lesson.

"Lapse in decorum, indeed. You've really gone and done it this time," she whispered into the cinnamon-scented air.

She was still staring at the batik ceiling, her dinner forgotten as she discarded one escape plan after another, when Marta's light tap came on the door.

LAUGHING AT another of Bill Patterson's amazingly rude, but equally hilarious jokes, Tucker waved the waitress away. "I'm done, but thank you."

She slid his dishes from the table, favoring him with a personal smile and an ample shot of her bountiful cleavage as she did so.

Miguez and Patterson both shook their heads. "Your first time in Vegas and you're sitting around with two old coots swapping cop stories. What's wrong with you, boy?'' Miguez joked. ''Didn't Jackson tell you anything about the women in this town?''

''Oh, we've heard stories,'' Tucker assured him with a wide grin. ''But pretty women are everywhere. These kinds of stories aren't.''

Patterson laughed and tapped out his cigarette. ''He's a goner, Mig.'' He looked to Tucker. ''You sure you don't want to think about heading up here for good? Focus like yours? All that training? Seems like such a waste.''

Tucker had already brushed them off several times. Not that he wasn't flattered. But before he could change the subject again, Mig's beeper went off.

Mig checked the message, then flipped open his phone and punched in a number. ''Fill me in,'' he said, then listened. His brows shot up. ''No shit. At the new place? Figures. I've said all along you can't mix sex and commerce without somebody getting hurt. I'll be there.'' He clicked the phone shut. ''Homicide at Blackstone's.''

Patterson's beeper went off a second later. ''Looks like I'm heading your way, too,'' he said as he checked the readout. He threw some bills on the table and shoved his chair back.

Mig looked at Tucker. ''Why don't you ride along? See what you're passing up.''

Tucker knew he was just being polite, but the offer was too tantalizing to pass up. ''Don't mind if I do.''

2

MISTY SHIFTED on the sultanlike raised dais and dragged a satin pillow in front of her breasts, wondering if she could be any more humiliated. "Certainly. You could have actually climaxed *on* the massage table." She shuddered and would have blushed again, if her skin wasn't already burnished and gleaming from the expert hands of her masseuse. Celandra. A woman.

Misty was more forward thinking than most, but really...a woman? That wasn't even a Misty Fortune fictional fantasy, much less a personal one of hers. Not that Celandra had given any indication she'd noticed her client's highly aroused state, her mission had only been to prepare her for Concubine 101. Misty was pretty certain she wasn't supposed to come during the prep phase. But Christ, the woman's hands had been bloody everywhere. Every. Where. It was a miracle really that she hadn't climaxed half a dozen times.

"Except damn Celandra moving her hands away just at the last possible moment," she grumbled. Every single time. No tip for her, Misty decided, rubbing her oiled thighs against the renewed twitch between them.

On the other hand, maybe she owed the nimble Celandra a coveted spot in her will after all. Because God only knew she'd succeeded in her mission. Misty felt like she was teetering on some monumental sexual precipice. Every inch of her skin was both relaxed and exquisitely hypersensitive. One particular inch was screaming for release. In fact, it might be a rather short tutorial session. Her partner had only to brush against any part of her and she'd likely dissolve into long moans of ecstasy.

She rubbed her thighs together again and shuddered in almost-there pleasure. "I should be so lucky." She sighed.

She looked around the chamber Marta had led her to after Celandra had finished with her. It wasn't the one she should have been in originally. Marta had mentioned something about it not being ready and had led her here instead. Wherever here was. With all the twists and turns, she had no idea where in the resort she was at this point.

But the walk had been worth it. The room was amazing really. An amalgam that was part sultan's lair, part Far Eastern enclave, with a little old English bordello thrown in for good measure. According to Marta, she would be the first one to…enjoy it, as this part of the resort had only recently been finished.

She wondered what he was going to look like, her tutor. Would he be Asian? Muscles like a martial arts expert, hands that had mastered arts of an entirely different sort? Or perhaps he'd have the smooth skin and bottomless black eyes of an Arab prince, with hands skilled enough to rule desert kingdoms…and her. Maybe he'd have the polished refinement of an aristocrat, with skin as pale as her own, and slender, clever fingers. A man who was an absolute gentleman in the front room, but who knew exactly what kind of wicked goings-on could be indulged in above stairs…and enjoyed them every chance he got.

Regardless, he was going to be hers, at least for the night, and together they would explore the kind of pleasures she'd only written about. She slowly pushed away the pillows she'd strategically moved to block key zones of her body—mostly the erogenous ones, though she'd already learned there were far more of those than she'd ever imagined. Which, considering her occupation, was really saying something.

She slid to what she thought might be a provocative pose, knees bent to the side, breasts thrust forward, back slightly arched. She tried what she thought might be a sultry look, but that ended on a spurt of laughter. Really, she wrote about femme fatales, but just because her inner heroine was teetering on the orgasmic cliffs of delight did not mean her outward appearance had changed any.

She was still awkwardly lanky, with legs that were too long and breasts that were too small. Her hair was a mass of wispy, unmanageable curls in an unexceptional shade of brown, framing pale English skin that tended to flush in splotches rather than a sexy glow. Although she had to admit Celandra had done a good job at enhancing the latter and diminishing the former. About the only thing she had going for her was her eyes, which were the unusual hue of her namesake stone. However, she doubted that would be the first thing he noticed. Or the second.

"Come now," she scolded herself. "You're a sultry concubine," she murmured, trying to get into the spirit. "A woman trained in the arts of pleasure. Men beg for your skilled attentions, fall at your feet in homage to your beauty." She tried not to snort…or look down at her rather indelicate size tens. She arched her back again, this time draping her arms over her head. She drew up one knee and let it dip across the other outstretched thigh.

Think concubine, think conqueror of men. A wanton seductress who can master any sexual situation, who can have any man exactly the way she wants him. Who can demand that any man take her in exactly the way she begs to be taken.

She thrust her breasts heavenward. "Come and get me," she growled.

TUCKER WANDERED down another corridor into the newly finished part of the resort, studying the map the Blackstone security team had provided him. The cameras weren't working in this area yet, but then, there were no guests sequestered here. However, he was sent to make sure no one else was hiding here, either. Considering the rather tricky layout of the resort, Mig. had done an admirable job in sealing off the area immediately surrounding the scene. Lucas Blackstone had been completely accessible and willing to do whatever was necessary to help. But the very private nature of his business had made the very access they needed—namely to the other guests who might have heard or seen something—next to impossible to accomplish.

A handful of the guests had left the premises before the police had arrived and many of the others had contacted legal counsel, refusing to speak until their attorneys were present to insure their privacy was not abused. The media was already encamped just beyond the now-closed gates at the end of the winding drive, distanced but by no means forgotten. Mig had taken over the forensic team, while the two homicide detectives assigned to the case had taken over the investigation. Patterson was representing the medical examiner's office, dealing with the body. Tucker had been pressed into service by the officers presently fanning out, searching for any additional guests who hadn't been accounted for.

He didn't mind the duty, only wishing he could do something more substantive to help out. At least he was getting an inside look at the place. And what a place it was. In his wildest dreams he couldn't have come up with anything like this.

Blackstone had spared no expense. Not in the richly detailed layout, the lavishly appointed rooms, the training of his staff—if the security team was anything to go by—or the extent of security he was installing. Tucker had also gotten wind of the rates, and while it appeared the guests got their money's worth, he still couldn't get past the fact that people would pay so much for what basically amounted to sex camp for adults.

He glanced at his map again and ducked into another grotto, then around yet another lagoon toward the cluster of rooms behind it. Each room had two entrances, to ensure privacy, he was sure, but also to maintain the fire code. The man really had thought of everything.

He used the house key card he'd been given and slipped it into the first door. He opened it quietly. The room was dark, as expected. He found the pressure pad and brought up the lights, and tried not to boggle at the array of, well…toys he supposed some would call them. If you were into that sort of thing. He did a cursory check under the bed—or rack he supposed was a better term—and in a few of the leather-covered cabinets, but found nothing. Nothing having to do with the investigation anyway. To each his own, he thought, closing the door behind him…and trying really hard not to imagine what one did with a two-headed dildo on a chain. Or why they'd want to even try.

He checked the next several rooms in the same manner, each of which had a completely different decorative theme. He'd actually been sort of intrigued with the one that had its own private lagoon right in the center of the room. There had been all sorts of tub toys for that one. Ones he'd actually be interested in playing with.

Other than piquing his curiosity though, nothing was out of place. He finished the last room and clicked on his radio. "Greywolf. Sector 12 is clear." He spoke as he ducked into the internal hallway, but noticed another alcove on his map with a door marked at the rear. "Wait, there's one more room."

"Copy. Report when it's clear."

It took a few seconds to find it, as it was behind another grotto in what initially looked like a wall of stone, but he finally found the curved entrance to a short recessed entryway. "Some people must really have some privacy issues," he muttered, wondering how many celebrities Blackstone's catered to. "Or government officials," he added with a wry smile.

He was still shaking his head as he slid his key into the slot and opened the door. He automatically went to touch the light pad before he realized that the lights were already on.

He immediately stilled and shifted to the side of the open door, inside the room.

"Halloo?"

The voice was cultured, British. And decidedly female. Tucker recovered quickly, but didn't respond. He was tucked behind what looked to be a hand-painted Japanese screen. Why hadn't security known someone was in this sector? Unless she was hiding. But why call out then? He peered through the slit between the panels, thinking maybe she'd been detained somehow, or that it was a trap of some kind. "Sweet Jesus," he murmured as he got a good look at the raised dais in the center of the room.

If this was a trap, it was a damn good one.

She was splayed, all dewy skin and wide eyes, across a pile of silk and satin. She certainly didn't look like she was being held against her will. Nor did she look like a homicidal maniac. But she was most definitely dangerous. All long glisteny limbs, aroused nipples and naked skin.

Maybe vacations weren't such a bad idea after all.

"I say, are you my...my— What *do* I call you?"

Turned on, was his immediate thought. Tucker cleared his throat...and the wild thoughts careening through his mind. Thoughts of what it would be like to be the man she was waiting for. Shucking his jeans and shirt and climbing over that pile of satin...and right into what she was so willingly offering.

It was clear she had no idea he wasn't a Blackstone employee. Not that he had much experience in anything like this setup, but his instincts told him she was simply a guest who had been put in this room by mistake and security hadn't been alerted. Now he had to come up with some way not to mortify her any more than she'd already be when he explained who he really was. He cleared his throat. "Ma'am, I'm terribly sorry, but—"

"I can't understand what you're saying, the screen is muffling your words. It's alright, you know, you can show yourself." It wasn't until she took a visibly steadying breath and pushed herself back into her centerfold position that he realized she wasn't as confident of the situation as she'd first appeared. He also realized that he was still staring at her.

He quickly shifted his gaze, but his body wasn't so easily diverted. "No, ma'am, you don't understand," he tried again. "I'm not your—whoever it is you're waiting for. I'm—"

She interrupted him with a light, somewhat forced laugh. "Is this part of the plan then? Am I to take the upper hand? Because, I must honestly tell you that I'd been made to understand it would be quite the opposite. At—at least for this first time." Her voice had faltered near the end. "Come, show yourself. If it's breaking some rule, I won't tell. But it would make things easier for me." Another shaky breath. "Please?"

Tucker sighed, hating the embarrassment he was about to cause. "I'm not with Blackstone's," he said clearly. "I'm assisting the LVMPD. There's been a problem here in the resort. I'm going to need you to cover up and come with me."

There was a gasp, then a sudden rustle of satin. "This isn't part of the...the plan then?" she asked weakly.

Tucker took a quick peek. She was wrapped in some thin paper silk-looking thing that was somehow almost more sinfully erotic than her nakedness. "No, ma'am. And I apologize for the interruption. I was told these rooms were empty and I wasn't expecting to find...what I found." He glanced through the screen again. She was tying the knot in her robe, so he stepped out from behind the screen, wishing he were just about anywhere else.

"The room I was supposed to be in wasn't ready, so Marta, that is, my assistant, brought me here. She must not have alerted my director to the shift. What happened?"

She was obviously mortified, but he didn't know what else to do except act as professional as possible—and deliver her to someone else's care as soon as possible. "If you'll follow me, I can explain on the way."

He turned for the door, pulling his radio out. "I've got a guest in room—" He looked at the small plaque next to the door in the hallway. "Twelve-A. Says she was moved here from another room. She's fine, but I need to know where to bring her."

WHILE HER INTRUDER spoke with God knew who, Misty tried to get a grip on what was going on here. She'd been so…ready. This intrusion was more than mortifying, it was an unwanted jolt of reality in the middle of the fantasy she'd so doggedly immersed herself in. Dammit, she'd been *ready*.

She yanked her belt tighter in frustration. Well, okay, as ready as she was ever likely to be. She'd never be able to do this again. She should have known it wasn't going to work, that something would happen. Embarrassment fueled her frustration, which turned into anger. "I don't understand, what kind of problem? Why were the police called?" she demanded of him, even though his back was still to her as he listened to the squawk of his radio.

Gripping the fabric closed at her throat and smoothing her other hand over her thighs to keep the paper-thin robe from flapping open, she was about to demand an answer from him again when he clipped his radio to his belt and turned to face her once again. Her mouth opened, but nothing came out as she got her first good look at him.

He was rather tall, very broad across the chest and shoulders. His legs were thick and long, made more so by the straight black jeans and western boots he wore as casually as the men on Wall Street wore pinstripes. It was too dimly lit to make out his eyes, other than they were dark. Smoky came to mind. His hair was a thick, inky black, cut short in a way that emphasized the Native American heritage clearly defined in the flat, angular planes of his cheeks and lips. *Damn,* she caught herself thinking, maybe she should have gone for the Warrior Abduction package after all.

"Are you sure you don't work here?" she blurted before clamping her lips together. Yet another momentary lapse. She seemed to be cursed with them ever since she'd touched down in this godforsaken city.

"You're not in any danger," he assured her.

A real shame, that, she couldn't help but think. Maybe she wasn't quite back in the land of harsh reality after all. Or maybe clinging to the fantasy was simply less humiliating.

"Is there anything else you need to take with you? I really need to clear you from this part of the building."

Misty sighed and unwillingly shook free of the last vestiges of the sensual fog she'd been so expertly wrapped in…and focused instead on what he was saying. "Clear out? Is there a fire? I didn't hear any alarms or—"

"No, ma'am, nothing like that." He stepped back and motioned to the door. "This way."

She didn't see where she had any choice. But now that her mortification and anger were ebbing…along with that delicious aroused state she'd been in, other questions occurred to her. Questions that needed answers before going one more step with him. She might be a transplanted Brit, but she'd quickly learned that New Yorkers adopted a wary attitude for good reason. ''Who are you? Are you security here?'' Then she remembered he'd said he didn't work for Blackstone's. ''Can I see some ID?''

He'd already been moving to the door, careful not to look directly at her. She should be thankful for that, and she was, but not enough to blindly trust him just because he was being a gentleman.

He paused and she thought she saw his shoulders move a bit as if he'd sighed. Had she caught him in some kind of lie then? She tensed, suddenly realizing just how alone she was. Privacy was a great thing, unless you needed help. She surreptitiously scanned the corners for security cameras, thinking maybe she could flag some help. Certainly with all the other myriad details Blackstone had thought to include in this place, he'd included a way to monitor— That thought stopped her cold. Considering what she should have been doing in this very room, at this very moment, the idea that some security guard could be watching from somewhere deep in the bowels of the resort was not exactly a heartening possibility. Not that she spied any cameras anyway.

She rubbed her arms as he turned around to face her. Was it her admittedly vivid imagination, or did he look nothing like any kind of security detail she'd ever seen? Nor did he look like any cop she'd ever seen, undercover or otherwise. Not that she knew all that much about undercover cops. She stopped rubbing her arms and tried to quickly determine the best way of handling this. Handling him.

A Misty Fortune heroine would disarm him with

her seductive charms, perhaps even seduce him, enjoy what favors he had to offer until he was limp with exhaustion, allowing her the chance to steal quietly away to safety.

As it turned out, while the idea held a great deal of appeal, she was far better writing a Misty Fortune heroine than being one.

"Your name," she demanded, her voice almost steady.

"Tucker Greywolf," he said immediately.

So her inner thighs twitched ever so slightly as that warrior-abduction scenario came back to her once again. She might have even had a glancing vision of him in full warrior headdress and warpaint, pulling her astride his stallion at a full gallop before—

"I'm assisting the LVMPD," he continued. "I'm actually a fire marshal from New Mexico, here for some forensic seminars." He reached in his back pocket and pulled out his wallet, flipping it open so he could see his badge.

"Fire marshal? But you said there wasn't a fire." That's what she said, but in her mind, she was seeing *Fire Marshal Greywolf, dragging her to safety from a burning building, then tearing her charred clothing off to make certain she was unharmed, only to be quite naturally overwhelmed by her obvious charms and—*

"No fire," he stated in that deep, flat way of his. "Really, ma'am—"

"Misty," she blurted, still clearing the images from her mind.

"I beg your pardon?"

Oh no, she thought a bit breathlessly, *I'd be the one doing all the begging.* Sweet Lord but the man had presence. "My name," she managed. "And I'm a *miss*." A miss who couldn't be any more pathetic, she thought ruefully. Apparently the aroused and ready part hadn't ebbed all that quickly. "Never mind," she quickly added, corralling her wayward hormones. "Just show me how to get back to my room." The poor man probably thought she was some sex-starved looney. At the moment, she wasn't too sure she wasn't living up to that assumption.

"I'm afraid that won't be possible," he said calmly, smoothly, in that liquid-honey voice of his. "The police will want to ask a few questions first."

Well, that last part took care of any lingering Misty Fortune heroine fantasies. Her entire body went cold. "The police? What on earth for?" It was one thing to have her sexual escapades interrupted by Warrior Marshal Man here, but quite another to even imagine parading in front of anyone else dressed like this. "I really think you must explain what is going on here."

"You're not in any trouble, but they'll want to ask you some questions. They're speaking to all the guests." He reached for her elbow without taking it, more as a "come on" kind of gesture. "They just need to clear every guest before anyone can leave. I'm sure everything will be fine."

She walked to the door, then stopped again. "Leave?" She spun around. "You mean they're shutting the place down?" That was it then. She wasn't ever going to get what she wanted. Hell, she couldn't even pay to get it. Talk about pathetic. This was some kind of celestial sign. One she should heed if she ever got such a crazy idea in her head ever again.

"I'm not sure what Mr. Blackstone will do, ma'am. I don't know what scope the investigation will encompass. I'm sure they'll answer all your questions, and don't worry, they're being very discreet."

She felt the splotches spring forth on her neck and chest. But she'd be damned if she went out like someone who had something to be ashamed of. With a toss of her head and a regal bearing befitting a graduate of Miss Pottingham's School of Grace and Charm, she floated past him into the hall. Her exit was only slightly flawed by having to stop and wait for him to lead the way, as she had no clue where she was in the maze of lagoons and grottoes that made up Blackstone's.

She stared at his broad, straight back as she followed behind him, determined not to say another word. She'd find out all she needed to know from the police. He'd used the word investigation. She wondered what kind. Drugs maybe? Whatever the case, she wasn't asking him. But she couldn't keep herself from imagining all sorts of possible scenarios. Occupational hazard.

What she couldn't explain was why her scenario possibilities had a lot more to do with the man in front of her doing various things to her as he got her out of danger, than with whatever intrigue had actually brought him here.

She stepped into the elevator, moving to the back corner, thankful when he turned his back to her again. His nice broad back. She stole a few glances at his profile, mirrored in the glassy tinted walls. So, maybe this trip wasn't a total wash after all, she thought, wheels beginning to spin. At the very least she just might have an idea for a hot new hero for her next Misty Fortune novel. She ducked her chin when he glanced toward the glassed wall...and smiled privately to herself.

My yes. He'd do.

3

TUCKER COULDN'T TAKE his eyes off of her.

She wasn't like anyone he'd ever met. Which, of course, wasn't saying much. Canyon Springs was hardly the crossroads of the world. By the time he left Vegas, he imagined it was entirely possible he'd have met a list of unique individuals. A long list.

But he still couldn't take his eyes off of her.

And not just because he'd seen her naked. Actually, she was more provocative to him now, entertaining questions from the police and asking some of her own, all while wearing nothing more than that silk wrapper. Yet, no one was ogling, no one was treating her with anything but the utmost respect. Partly professionalism, sure, but he was willing to bet that only went so far. No, the reason they were handling her like a queen was that, paper-thin robe notwithstanding, she emanated a somewhat regal bearing. Gazing coolly from those amazing gemstone eyes of hers, she sat in a padded office chair like a ruler might sit in a velvet throne. The clipped British accent only underscored the whole aura. He wondered if she was aware of it, manipulating it for her own purposes when it suited her, or if it was simply second nature, something she was completely unaware of.

He studied her from across the small office in between sips of coffee. Mig and Patterson were still in the suite with the victim, collecting evidence. Tucker could have caught a cab back to the hotel, but Mig had sent word out that they'd give him a free pass through the media throng if he wanted to hang around. At the moment, there was nowhere else he wanted to be.

He would have liked to check the murder site out himself, but he was both well outside his jurisdiction and his real arena of knowledge in this particular situation. Not too many aging movie queen socialites getting murdered while involved in kinky sex games back in Canyon Springs. Besides, it gave him the opportunity to watch Misty Fortune.

Amethyst Fortuna Smythe-Davies, to be completely accurate. Hell of a name, that. He could see why she went by her nom de plume. He'd been surprised when she'd told the officers she was a novelist. Erotica, no less. Despite the circumstances under which they'd met, he'd never have imagined her doing that. Something about that cool regal bearing of hers. He made a mental note to look up a title or two. Shouldn't be too hard. Apparently they were all bestsellers.

He topped off his coffee and leaned against the corner of the short hall that led from the office to the door. Just out of her direct line of vision, but still able to watch her eyes, her mouth, her body language, as she asked and answered questions.

She was polite, if distant, although that might have been the uppercrust accent giving that impression. He smiled into his coffee. Anyone seeing her now, even in that wrapper, would never in a million years imagine her splayed amongst those satin pillows, all ready to accept a stranger into her arms…and between her legs. Her slender hands and elegant fingers held the paperlike silk closed at her throat and over her knees. Not a speck of pale flesh peeked out, and yet Tucker was one breath away from arousal every time her lips parted.

Surprisingly, despite her reserve, she'd asked a good many questions of her own. Of course, the detectives had been circumspect in giving out any details of the murder, but at the same time, they seemed to be a bit taken with the fact that she was a well-known author. An author whose subject matter lent itself well to the surroundings. If Tucker wasn't mistaken, they were a bit flattered to be the subject of her research, which was most certainly what she was doing.

He wondered if that was also what she'd been doing back in the satin pillow room. Maybe her stories weren't entirely fictional. Or even partly. Which launched a whole new train of thought that was abruptly cut off when she stood with a serene smile and thanked the detectives for their time.

Who'd been interrogating whom, he wondered, as the detectives both nodded and grinned and did everything but ask for an autograph. Tucker turned to toss his cup in the trash, hiding his own grin. Not that she'd directed so much as a blink or nodding glance in his direction since taking her seat with the detectives. But she'd have to now, since he was blocking the way out.

She turned back to the officers before taking more than a step. "Are the guests expected to check out this evening, then?"

The detectives had been in the process of taking their seats again, but both straightened immediately. Tucker privately wondered if they'd bow and scrape, too. Probably, if they thought it would get them anywhere with her. Admittedly, he probably would, too. For the same reason.

"No, ma'am," the older detective, Riggins, answered her. "However, since we won't need to question you again, you are free to leave the premises if you wish."

The other detective, Faulkner, younger, with a far too serious expression, shifted forward to add, "You might want to wait until morning however."

Misty merely raised a brow in response. Tucker couldn't help thinking how different she was here, in this room. How much more assured she was. Made him wonder just what kind of adult camp games she'd signed up for in that other room. She'd been uncertain there, on edge. Then he recalled that she'd said she hadn't expected to be the one taking charge. Hmmm. Maybe when men found out what she did for a living, they expected her to be the dominant one between the sheets. Maybe her fantasy was to give up that burden, have her needs catered to for a change. Or maybe the men she met felt too much pressure to live up to her image. Performance anxiety and all that.

So, had she been acting back in that room? Those

steadying breaths, the slight wobble in her tone? Had that all been part of the scenario she'd paid for?

Looking at her now, it was hard to believe otherwise.

"I understand the media is camped en masse outside the gates," Detective Faulkner finished. "And we've sealed off the helipad until our investigation here is done."

"As I don't have my private chopper with me, that won't be a problem," she said, dry humor surfacing for the first time.

"We'll be giving the press a statement later tonight," Riggins offered. "I imagine they will head off to make their deadlines after that. By morning they'll be onto something else."

Tucker thought the detective was being a bit disingenuous with that remark. He didn't think the media was going anywhere and he doubted the detectives really did either. The murdered woman, Patsy Denton, had been a well known B-movie actress back in the fifties, known more for her teenage sex kitten body than her acting abilities. However, she'd proven to be a shrewd businesswoman, and for the past several decades had been better known as a socialite, sometime political activist and generous philanthropist. Her husband, Drew Ralston, at forty-eight was almost twenty years her junior. He was a resort developer and occasional high stakes gambler. Apparently she'd gambled with some high stakes as well. And paid with her life.

The media would sink both claws deep into this one and it would be a while before they shook loose.

"Thank you, gentlemen," Misty was saying. "For the time being, I'll be staying."

She turned again and it was only when she drew closer that Tucker noticed her knuckles were white from the grip she had on her robe. So…was the regal queen part the act then? He found that harder to believe. She was far too good at it. But the instant she noticed the direction of his gaze, her grip visibly relaxed. The slight vibration of the silk, however, told another story. Her fingers trembled.

Why? Nerves from talking to the police? She could have fooled him. Something to hide? He didn't think so, neither did the cops. So, what then? What made Amethyst Fortuna Smythe-Davies, aka Misty Fortune, erotica author, tremble?

"Do you have one?" he asked as she paused, waiting for him to move to one side of the short hallway so she could pass.

She finally looked directly at him. How eyes so passionately colored could come across so cool and distant he had no idea, but she managed it. There was ice in her tone as well.

"Have one of what?" she asked, the British accent so clipped now he was surprised he wasn't left bleeding.

"A private chopper," he asked, flashing a smile, finding himself wanting to bait her and yet protect her at the same time. "You must have sold a bunch of books."

"No, I don't," she responded flatly. "And yes," she said, her lips curving just the slightest bit, "I have."

His grin widened and a third urge joined the others. This one decidedly carnal. He doubted she'd be flattered by any of them.

As if in silent response, her half smile disappeared. She pulled her robe a bit more tightly about her slender throat, and shifted slightly. "If you'll please let me pass, I'd like to return to my room."

Grin firmly in place, Tucker bowed slightly and silently shifted to one side. The path was narrow and she had to turn slightly to avoid brushing against him as she passed. He could have made it easier, probably should have. A gentleman would have. Apparently that wasn't one of the urges she brought out in him.

Behind him, Riggins was on the phone and Faulkner had flipped on the small television set in the corner to see what the evening news was making of the situation. Because it had taken a while to find her, there was no one else waiting to be questioned. Once the detectives sat down with Mig and company and compared notes, there would be other interviews. Likely those would take place at the station, or in a lawyer's office.

Tucker watched her slip quietly into the hall. He'd probably never see her again. He wasn't involved in the investigation, had no reason to contact her. In fact, he should track down Mig and see about getting that ride back to the hotel. Maybe get a chance to learn more about what was going on, what they'd found out. That's what he should have been focused on, what he was here for. To learn.

What he did, however, was step forward at the last possible second to catch the door before it snapped shut. He had no idea what he was going to say to her, he just knew he wasn't okay with letting her walk away. He ducked into the hall, hoping to catch a glimpse of her before she turned a corner—and almost steamrolled right over top of her.

There was a muffled thump as she tried to avoid the collision and hit the opposite wall instead. She swore something that sounded like "God's balls," then straightened quickly away from the wall, and him.

"I'm sorry, I didn't realize you were still right by the door," Tucker said, instinctively reaching for her to steady her.

She moved back, her expression making it quite clear she was steady enough thank-you-very-much. "I—uh, I was merely, um—" She broke off and pushed her fingers through her hair before dropping them a bit self-consciously and straightening her shoulders.

Not so steady when caught off guard, Tucker noted with interest.

"Can't find your way home?"

Color bloomed very becomingly on her cheeks, and not so becomingly across the base of her neck, where her hand fluttered as if aware that reaction might occur. Oddly, he was more attracted to the fluttering hands and splotchy neck than he was the rosy perfection of her English complexion.

"I simply need to use the phone and contact my…contact the desk." She drew herself up, but kept her hand at her neck, on the pretense of clutching her robe closed, he thought. Except that robe was so tightly belted nothing short of a hurricane was going to rip it open.

A hurricane or the attentions of a very determined lover.

He ducked that vision, but not the smile it brought to his lips. "I have a map of the resort layout. If you tell me your room number, I'll be happy to escort you."

"That won't be necessary."

"Fine. But with everything that's happened tonight, it might take management a while to send someone. Several of the guests were— Well, let's just say they didn't take the news that someone had been murdered on the premises as well as you did."

"What exactly are you insinuating?"

She was the oddest mix of stiff upper lip and nervous twitches. He was beginning to think both performances were a part of who she really was. How intriguing. "Nothing. In fact, I admired the way you handled the whole thing."

"Indeed," she said, more to herself than to him.

"Indeed," he repeated. "You know, I won't bite." At her questioning look, he directed his gaze to the death grip she had on her robe.

"I'm not accustomed to socializing in little more than a cellophane wrapper."

"But handling police interrogations are no problem at all apparently. At least, you'd never have guessed otherwise from your performance in there."

The slightest of smiles quirked her lips as she studied his face. "I'm not so sure I believe you. About the biting."

"You totally fascinate me." He saw no reason not to just admit that up front.

The smile faltered, the grip tightened.

But he didn't back down. "One moment you're the royal queen, entertaining her subjects. The next you're like…well, I can't describe it really. Uncertain of yourself. Though I can't imagine how or why."

She shifted the slightest step farther away from him, but didn't directly comment on his evaluation other than to say, "Yes, well, the circumstances here are a bit far removed from the typical, aren't they? Tends to make a person behave in ways somewhat out of step with the norm. Not all that fascinating really. Now, if you'll excuse me." She motioned with her head to the office door, which he was now blocking.

"Misty—"

She shot him a look of surprise.

"I was standing right in the room. I might not be directly involved in the investigation, but I do know your name." And your occupation, he thought, but didn't say. As it was, she probably thought he was another slug, interested more by what she did, and in this case where she was presently doing it, than who she was. Well, he admitted to being intrigued by all that, but his interest had been sparked long before he knew anything about her job. Of course, that might have had something to do with the fact that she'd been stark naked at the time.

"Exactly how is it you came to be assisting this department? You said you were in town for a fire marshal class or something? I'm surprised they've allowed such familiarity.''

And here he was, wishing she'd allow him a bit more familiarity. "Professional courtesy. The classes are in forensic investigation. I was having a late dinner with two of the instructors when they were called to the scene. I tagged along."

"And was it professional courtesy that had you lurking behind the screen in my room?"

"I wasn't lurking." Leering a little maybe, he thought, but hell, what red-blooded man wouldn't have? He didn't attempt to make that distinction, however. "And I am sorry for putting you in such an awkward situation."

She gave him a look. "You seem to be very good at that."

He smiled. "Yeah, apparently I am."

"Yes. Well." She shifted slightly. "Don't let me keep you from whatever duty it was that sent you racing out of the door."

"Actually, I came racing out the door to catch you."

"Did the officers have something else they wanted?"

He looked directly at her, waited until her eyes met his. "No. But I did."

She blinked. Several times.

"As I said before. You fascinate me. And it's not the location, or what you're wearing, or even what you do for a living." He raised his hand as she raised her eyebrow. "I didn't miss much."

"No, I don't believe you do."

"I won't lie. All of that is interesting. I'm an investigator, I can't help being curious. But that's not why I ran out here. I'm not all lathered up because I think you're a hot piece looking for some action for your next book."

Those eyes of hers widened momentarily, before her regal reserve once again settled around her like a well-worn mantle. "So, I'm not a 'hot piece' then? Well, that's certainly a bit of news. I'm extremely relieved to hear it."

Tucker felt color rise in his cheeks and tried to recall the last time a woman had ever made him blush. He'd been maybe seven. "My finesse is lacking. I was trying to explain that I wasn't jumping to conclusions based on circumstantial evidence."

Her lips remained flat, but the slightest of twinkles lit her eyes. The transformation from icy gem to glittering jewel was captivating. "You're right about the finesse," she said. "Pity."

"You should do that more often," he murmured.

"What? Put down men who make a habit of eating their own feet? I do that too often myself to make sport of it."

"You didn't seem to have a problem handing it to me."

The twinkle glistened again and her lips curved almost in spite of themselves. "It comes more naturally when I'm particularly inspired."

Tucker smiled. "I suppose I should be flattered then."

"Quite the optimist, aren't you?"

Tucker leaned against the wall and folded his arms. "There. That's what I was talking about."

She looked about, confused.

He very tentatively reached out and touched her chin, turning her face slowly back to his.

She stiffened, eyed him warily.

"I really don't bite."

"I'd really rather you didn't—"

"It's the twinkle," he said, quietly interrupting her.

"I beg your pardon?" She shifted her chin away from his touch.

He very purposely brushed his finger along the curve of her chin again. The finest of shivers rewarded the risk. "Actually, I think I'll be the one doing the begging."

Her lips quirked again and he swore she almost laughed. "Who'd have thought it," she murmured. Then to him, she added, "You're really—"

"Fascinating?"

"I don't believe that was the word I was going to use."

"Your eyes," he said, quite seriously. "They are amazing. But I'm sure you've been told that a hundred times. A thousand. Such a passionate color. And yet you have this way of making them so cool and distant." He smiled. "Like right now."

She went to move away completely, but he turned and boxed her in against the wall. He wasn't touching any part of her, but she could slip out to either side.

She didn't.

She didn't look at him directly either.

He noticed she was breathing more rapidly by the

rise and fall of her chest. His own was a bit accelerated as well.

"But when you relax, let your guard down," he went on, as if they were having a casual conversation, "they light up with this…well, twinkle. Takes my breath away." And yet there was nothing remotely casual happening between them right now. She might be a mystery to him, one he'd like to solve. But the source of that snap, crackle, pop in the air was no mystery at all.

He knew sexual tension when he felt it. And, from the way her pupils slowly expanded when she turned her head to look directly at him…so did she.

"Will you be staying in Vegas?" he asked.

She said nothing, but kept her gaze on his.

"I'll be here the rest of the week," he said, then waited. Determined to wait as long as it took to get a response from her.

"Me, too," she said finally, the words barely a murmur.

"Four days." It was both statement…and request.

"Four."

"Before we go our own way, back to our own worlds, never to cross paths again."

She stared at him for the longest time, but said nothing. Neither did she move away.

He lifted a hand, surprised to find that he was the one with the tremor this time. He slowly stroked a blunt-tipped finger along the side of her face. Her skin was as fine and smooth as the porcelain he'd compared it to. So incredibly delicate he wondered how careful he'd have to be not to bruise it. "For those four days," he said very quietly, "I'd like for our worlds to collide. A little. A lot. I don't care. Well, that's a lie. I know what I want."

Her pupils exploded then, jewels flashed, sparked, and he grew hard. Harder anyway.

"But I'll take your company any way you're comfortable sharing it," he finished.

"You'll press," she said and he wasn't sure if it was a question…or capitulation.

"You'll want me to."

"You're very certain of yourself."

"About some things."

"And if I say no?"

He lifted his hands, but kept his body close. "We walk away." He grinned then, despite the fact that his heart was hammering and his body felt like a live wire had been introduced into his bloodstream. Then he let a slightly shaky finger drop to the full center of her bottom lip. "It's up to you whether or not we're smiling, bodies spent, heads full of fond memories, when we do."

He let his hand drop away completely then, spent an agonizingly long moment staring at the spot he'd touched, wanting to taste it more than he wanted his next breath, before finally moving away from her. It took every ounce of willpower he owned, and a few more he had to take out on loan.

She took a moment to steady herself, then moved past him and put her hand on the office doorknob.

Was she really going to just walk away? he wondered. Just like that?

He wasn't used to the sudden sense of desperation

he felt. Which was probably why he blurted, "Can I call you then?" He'd never been in this position, of having to beg for attention. Maybe it was good for him. He wasn't so sure. He only knew that in that moment, he'd willingly sacrifice his ego and just about anything else on the chance she'd say yes. He didn't analyze why that was, why she was different. He saved that sort of deep thinking for crime scenes. Passion was supposed to be easier.

She stepped halfway through the door and he realized she really was going to leave without answering him. He wasn't sure what his next move should be. Walk away? Or continued pursuit?

But she turned then, and looked at him. "I'll think about it." Then she shut the door in his face.

He let his forehead drop until it thunked on the wall next to the door. "She'll think about it, she says." *And then what?* he wanted to yell through the door.

She had him literally tied in knots. "Hell, you started it," he grumbled, then pushed away from the wall. He gave the door a hard stare, but it didn't open. Nor did he go after her.

Not yet.

He turned and headed down the hall instead, thinking he'd find Mig and Patterson. Immerse himself in a good crime scene. Those he understood.

Women on the other hand…? Maybe murder was easier.

4

APPARENTLY EVEN MURDER didn't keep the Blackstone staff from their duties.

Misty had been half hoping her long cold dinner would still be in her room when she finally wound her way back to it. But the table was clear, her sheets had been turned back and the only food awaiting her was the chocolate rose on her pillow.

She was surprisingly ravenous. It would seem that police interrogation spiked her appetite.

She closed her eyes against the immediate image that took shape in her mind…and it wasn't either of the intrepid Las Vegas P.D. detectives. No, as intimidating as the entire procedure had been, as admittedly fascinated as she'd become by the macabre turn of events, as worried as she should have been by the fact that a killer was on the loose…none of those things were responsible for the sudden hunger that filled her.

Tucker Greywolf.

The way he'd looked at her, the words he'd spoken, the way he'd touched her… He was like a subconscious inquisition that wouldn't leave her alone.

I know what I want.

His words echoed inside her. As did her instinctive

response. She knew what she wanted, too. Couldn't stop thinking about it, imagining what it would be like. Those large hands on her body, that mouth of his, so smug, so certain. He'd do things to her…he'd let her do things to him. She knew it. It had been so clear when she'd looked into his eyes. She didn't need to pay someone here at Blackstone's. She could simply take him up on his offer. Take him. Period.

She would learn everything she wanted to know and more. He wouldn't even have to teach, he'd only have to set her loose on his body. She'd take it from there. He was quite…inspiring.

She smiled and shook her head. And here she thought people never met like they did in her books. The entire situation had been the perfect Misty Fortune set up. Two people in a place out of time, out of sync with their day to day lives. Tossed together in circumstances so beyond their normal experience that anything seems possible. Probable. And all of it at a resort that catered to fulfilling sexual fantasies.

Food. Not sex. With Tucker. Food, that's the only hunger she should worry about appeasing at the moment. She debated calling Marta back and asking if she could still get something to eat at this late hour, but ultimately decided against it. She was more unsettled than hungry anyway. Besides, Marta had been unnaturally subdued when she'd come to escort her back to her room. Misty imagined murder in the workplace would do that to a person, but she had to wonder if Marta hadn't also been called on the carpet for not reporting what room she'd ultimately put Misty in.

Lucas Blackstone, whom she'd only met briefly, didn't strike her as the type to let something like that slide, even in the midst of a murder investigation.

Work. That was always a good panacea for whatever ailed her. She dug out the small journal she kept in her purse. Which was more satchel than purse, actually, but while she'd grudgingly followed Blackstone protocol and left her laptop behind, her cell phone turned off and her Palm Pilot in hibernation mode, she never went anywhere without paper and pen. Inspiration had a way of sneaking up on her at the oddest moments.

Too many times she'd come up with the perfect snippet of dialogue, devised the most stunning descriptive passage, only to lose it during the interim between thought and locating something to write it down on. She'd initially tried a mini recorder, but the sound of her own voice was always at odds with how she heard things in her head, so she'd reverted to the timeless reliability of pen and paper.

She curled up on the bed, mindless now of the luxury surrounding her. Her focus was entirely inward. All the stimulation of her sensually drenching day, coupled with the sudden tension of the investigation, then Tucker's intrusion right into the middle of it all, might have been overwhelming in reality…but she had no problem turning the chain of events into fantasy. Images in her mind became words on the paper. The scenes unfolded swiftly, so detailed, one after the other, she couldn't write fast enough. By the time she reached the climax of the story, she was squirming for release herself.

Always a sign she'd accomplished what she'd set out to deliver.

But when it came to finishing the scene, somehow the flow of words dried up as if turned off by the handle of a faucet. She didn't push. Instead she tossed the journal on the bed and headed to the bathroom, thinking a shower might offer some solace. And maybe some release, she thought guiltlessly, remembering the hand-held unit attached to the shower head.

But as she stood beneath the pulsing spray, it quickly became clear that a jet of hot water, no matter how cleverly manipulated, was not going to bring her relief. Much less the release that was now like a nagging throb between her legs. Only now it had nothing to do with the ministrations of anyone on the Blackstone staff…and everything to do with the dark-eyed warrior of a fire marshal who'd stalked into her life a few hours ago.

Wrapped in a towel, she went back to the bedroom, thinking sleep would simply have to save her. But one glance at the journal tossed amidst the silk, with its freshly entered story so torridly taunting her, and she knew bed was the last place she'd find peace. Alone anyway.

Her gaze drifted beyond her patio door to her private indoor lagoon. The detectives hadn't said anything about staying in her room. Besides, the lagoon was accessible only through her room. Though, now that she thought about it, there was likely another entry somewhere in the jungle foliage that surrounded it for maintenance purposes. She moved to the French doors, then beyond them.

If it wasn't safe, surely the police would have evacuated the resort. They seemed pretty certain the killer was no longer on the premises. She shivered, but continued to draw closer to the lagoon, lured by the tendrils of steam drifting off the surface.

She chose the first bottle of scented oil from the small basket by the stone stairs that led down into the sprawling pool. A few drops and the misty air took on the spicy allure of vanilla. She dropped her thin robe on the chaise and stepped into the heated water. She swam to where a thin waterfall poured into the deep end with a quiet thrum. Standing beneath the gentle stream, Misty felt each and every water droplet splash and bounce off her skin. Her eyes drifted shut as she tipped her head back and let the clear water stream through her hair.

In her mind's eye, he came through the French doors, across the patio, stopping amidst the fronds and foliage, captivated by the look of her, welcoming the feel of the water as it cascaded over and caressed her every naked curve. She didn't open her eyes, merely felt his presence, let the idea of his watching her take hold, enhance the primal pleasure she'd already immersed herself in.

Back arched, her hands slid over slick skin, slipped over breasts that ached for a firmer hand, between legs that begged for something more substantial than her slender fingers. Her climax was a raw thing, leaving her panting and a bit shaken. When she finally stopped trembling, she blinked her eyes open, almost surprised to find the spot by the pool empty. He'd felt so incredibly real to her, in her fantasy.

That fantasy could be incredibly real, she taunted herself as she slipped beneath the surface and willed the echoing throb between her legs to diminish. With long, slow strokes, she swam back to the steps. She didn't bother to dry off, just plucked her thin robe off the chaise and went back to her bedroom. She tossed the journal aside, knowing she wasn't going to share what she'd just experienced with pen or paper, much less with her readers. She couldn't even let herself think about it too clearly in the privacy of her own mind.

It hadn't been too private out in the lagoon, she thought. In fact, it was the very public nature of the fantasy, with her audience of one, that had driven her to such a strong climax. She'd been alone, and yet not alone. And her solitude right now felt amplified because of that paradox. *You don't have to be alone.*

He was likely long gone by now. *Besides, you've built him up to a fantasy now.* He'd never match up, and then there'd be disappointment all around. Best to leave him to her fantasies. He'd certainly more than fulfilled his potential there. She closed her eyes, willing sleep to come and take her, release her from thinking about him, from what to do about him, or whether there was anything to be done about him.

Four days. Before we go our own way, back to our own worlds, never to cross paths again.

His words, so clear in her mind, chased away sleep. He'd been so confident that he could give her what she wanted. And yet, he didn't know her. Answers to questions, a police interrogation, that's what he knew of her. How could he know what *she* wanted?

I know what I want.

She shivered, remembering the look in his eyes when he'd said that. And maybe that was all that was important. That he understood his own wants. She wished she were so confident. She wasn't sure she could fulfill her own wants, much less any of his.

She rolled to her back, forcing her thoughts to the real world. What *was* she going to do tomorrow? Regardless of whether Blackstone intended to fulfill his obligation to his guests, she felt that her interlude here was over. She didn't want to stay here now. Her thoughts were too corrupted by everything that had happened, her fantasy bubble burst.

Replaced by a whole new fantasy. One that had nothing to do with what the resort had to offer.

Blackstone would likely refund her money or allow another stay at a later date. She rolled to her side, staring sightlessly into the darkness. Would she come back? She kicked at the silk sheets, damp from her swim, until she lay bare. Did she still want what this place had to offer?

Yes. And no.

Yes, she still wanted to experience her fantasies, the things she wrote about. And she wanted the freedom to do so safely, with no judgments, no strings, no repercussions. But did she want some nameless, well-trained Blackstone employee to teach her how to reach those dizzying heights of carnal delight?

No. Not anymore.

Maybe it was the fact that murder had been committed here. Such a brutal reality in a place where only fantasy was supposed to reign. And yet, her other option was what? Go back to New York? Back to her private fantasies, written in seclusion amidst the frenzy of a very public city?

A city that was a world away from a sexy fire marshal who spent his days keeping people safe in a small, southwestern town.

I'd like for our worlds to collide.

He'd offered her no strings. No repercussions. Left it up to her to dictate what they did with each other, to each other, how far they'd go. He'd push. And he was right, she'd want him to.

Four days. Four nights. She wasn't due back in New York for another six. That would give her two days to detox, deal with whatever she'd done—or wished she hadn't—and move on.

She rolled over and picked up the phone, pressed the button for her director before she could analyze all the reasons why this was a bad idea. Beginning with the safety issue—yeah, he was a public servant, but he was in a distant town, serving his own needs at the moment, a stranger to her without any privacy or satisfaction guarantees.

Yet, when Janece's calm, soothing voice picked up on the other end, asking if she needed anything, Misty heard herself say, "Yes, have the detectives left yet?" She held her breath, felt her lungs ache from the pressure, even though it couldn't have been more than a second or two before she got her answer. The breath left her in a crushing whoosh. Too late.

"No," she said, feeling an unreasonable anger surge inside her. As if it had been all his fault she'd taken this long to figure out what it was that she wanted. "That's alright. Thank you anyway."

She hung up the phone, very carefully, then gave into the now self-directed rage and beat up her pillow. "Sod it. Always a day late and an orgasm short. You'd think you'd have learned by now to take life by the balls, instead of letting it kick you there instead."

It was hours before sleep rescued her.

SHE WOKE EARLY, unrested, feeling edgy because of it. At least, that's where she laid the blame. She made the decision to leave right after breakfast. No point in belaboring things any longer. She informed Marta as soon as she arrived. The older woman took the information in stride and left to see to the details. Misty refused her offer to send someone to do her packing, too irritable to feel worthy of that kind of pampering today.

After a session in Janece's private office, where she'd so recently checked in, full of apprehension about what she would do while inside these plush walls, Misty went out front where a limo awaited to take her directly to the airport. She'd turned down their offer of another stay at a later date, deciding she'd simply chalk this whole thing up to an interesting weekend diversion and be thankful for the new flow of ideas it had brought to the surface—and not just sexual ones.

The edginess and neediness that refused to go away, well, she'd lived with those for years. She'd live with them again.

The driver was already stowing her bags when she came out front. She got into the back without waiting for him to assist her. Maybe she would take something else back with her as well, she thought. The determination to push a bit harder when it came to matters of sex, not to be afraid when opportunities presented themselves, to risk looking the fool, if it got her the experience she wanted to have. She leaned her head back on the soft leather and closed her eyes, trying to imagine asking any of her recent dates to do such things to her…or allow her to try things on them. Her smile was both dry and weary.

The downside of working alone. It made it that much harder to meet men. The ones she did meet, at museum functions, charity benefits, the corner coffee shop, all seemed to ultimately fall into two categories. Those who tried too hard to be what they thought a Misty Fortune hero would be. And those who were hoping she'd teach them how to be a Misty Fortune hero.

In fact, she'd long since stopped telling her dates what she did for a living. Saved them both from a great deal of strain and tension. Not to mention the possibility of a trashy tabloid story detailing how woefully inadequate the famous erotica author was in private. She laughed at herself.

Maybe she should try the club scene again, look for that dark stranger. She shuddered, and not in carnal anticipation. The reality was, she'd never once met a man in a crowded sweaty nightclub that made her want to get naked and have wild, uninhibited, no strings sex. She supposed it was the Brit in her. A part of her staid upbringing that even New York City hadn't been able to subvert.

The driver clicked the door shut and glanced in the rearview mirror. "To the airport, miss?"

Yes, she thought with a disappointed sigh. To the airport. To New York. To her tastefully decorated apartment, in her tastefully decorated life. To her fantasy world with her fantasy lovers who would forever be the only ones who truly knew what she wanted.

No.

One-night stands with sweaty lounge lotharios would never appeal to her. But there was a four-night stand offer on the table. Made by the only stranger she'd ever considered letting take her up against the nearest wall. No questions asked.

So what if it was location and circumstance, decadence and a day spent heightening her own awareness to aching extremes, that had made him seem so perfect for her purposes?

She asked the question before she could second guess herself into safe silence. "Do you happen to know what location the forensic team was called in from, before they came out here last night?"

She saw his perfectly smooth brow furrow slightly. "I beg your pardon, miss?"

"Several men on the forensic squad had been teaching seminars in town. Do you happen to know where they are holding these classes?"

It was clear on his face that he knew. After all, what else had the drivers, all employed by Blackstone's, had to talk about last night while waiting to be interviewed? It was also clear that he was uncomfortable revealing anything that smacked of a confidence. He was trained to drive and keep his mouth shut—at least to paying guests and the prying eyes of outsiders.

She was, at the moment, a bit of both. "Never mind," she said after his hesitation had dragged out an uncomfortable second too long. "But there's been a change in plans. Could you take me into town instead?" She had the full refund of her trip weighing down her bank account. She could easily afford a night's stay at even the nicest resort. Or four nights as the case may be. She named the first one that came to mind. If they didn't have a room, she'd look until she found one that did. "The Bellagio, please."

The driver, once again smooth of brow and unreadable of face, merely nodded and pulled silently away from the curb.

Empowered by her impulsive decision, pleased that she'd acted on it, Misty didn't look back at Blackstone's. She was too busy devising her plan. After all, writing wasn't entirely imagination and fantasy. Her characters had backgrounds and occupations, her stories had locations, all of which were grounded in reality. For those facts, she did research. Lots of research.

Certainly she could find out where the Las Vegas Metropolitan Police Department was holding a few forensics classes.

TUCKER STARED unseeing at the grisly photographs that flicked by on the overhead. Bullet exit wounds and the corresponding splatter marks on walls, floors

and furniture were the subject of the moment. Yet all
he saw were those dark violet eyes, debating, deciding
and ultimately shutting him out.

He couldn't stop thinking about her. He'd spent the
remainder of the night trying to talk himself out of
going back for her. It had just been the unusual way
they'd met, the city of sin seducing him as the hotel
valet had predicted, making him think it was perfectly
normal to offer four days of sex to a woman he'd just
met. Under circumstances that could hardly be de-
scribed as social.

He gnawed on the end of his pen, drummed his
fingers on his thigh, tried like hell to pay attention to
the instructor.

It didn't matter now. He'd given up the fight and
any remaining shred of dignity he had and called
Blackstone's this morning. She'd checked out. Decision final.

She was a celebrity of sorts. A published author. It
wouldn't be hard to track her down. But even as he
thought it, he rejected the idea and admonished himself for even going there. Christ, you'd think he
hadn't been laid in months the way he was panting
after this woman.

Truth of the matter was, though, if getting laid was
all he was after, he could slip his room number to the
waitress from the restaurant. It wasn't sex he was after. Okay. Lie. It *was* sex, but sex specifically with
Amethyst Fortuna Smythe-Davies.

*Put a restraining order on the libido, Greywolf,
and get back to the matter at hand.*

He looked up at the overhead projector again, just

in time to see the instructor shut it off and ask for any remaining questions. Normally he'd have a list of them. Today, he just wanted to get out of there. Regroup, get something to eat, hit the roulette tables. Maybe swing by the restaurant. Normally he wasn't much on business trip flings, but maybe that's exactly what he needed to clear this idiot possessed gotta-have-her thing from his head.

Lost in thought, the instructor had to grab his arm to get his attention as he passed him on his way out of the room. "Mr. Greywolf?"

"I'm sorry," he said, stopping short. With a brief smile, he added, "Mind was elsewhere."

The instructor chuckled. "Yeah, I noticed."

Tucker had the grace to flush slightly. The class had been relatively small, less than two dozen people. Still, he hadn't realized he'd been so obviously distracted. "I apologize. It wasn't you. Normally, I—"

His grin widened. "I heard. Million question man."

Tucker smiled. "I'm developing a bad rap apparently."

"No, quite the opposite. Mig tells me he tried to talk you over to the dark side, have fun in the desert with us. He told me to take up where he left off."

Tucker laughed. "A conspiracy. Sorry to let you down."

"Who said we're done? As a matter of fact, Mig asked if you wanted to join us later on, at the lab. We're going over some of the evidence. You mentioned to him last night that you'd trained in crime scene photography. We'd be interested in getting your perspective on a few things.''

Tucker looked more than a little skeptical. "A few classes with no practical application hardly makes me the go-to guy here.''

The instructor—Ted something or other, Tucker recalled—shrugged. "I heard it was more than a few classes. Besides, we're always open to fresh points of view. Sometimes those are the ones that make us look at things a different way. You interested?''

In getting an up-close look at the LVMPD's forensic lab? Was he kidding? And what better way to divert his mind from the odd hold Misty had on his every other thought than by losing himself in a scientific playground?

"Very interested. I need to run upstairs to my room, drop this stuff off.''

Ted nodded, pleased. "Great, I'll follow you up, give me more time to talk you into staying.''

Tucker just nodded, thinking that once again fact ruled over fiction. And that's all his proposed adventure with Ms. Smythe-Davies was ever going to be. Fiction.

5

MISTY WAS ALMOST more nervous now, fully dressed and in charge of her surroundings, than she had been naked and oiled in that room at Blackstone's. A room, she reminded herself, where he'd seen her in all her gleaming glory.

"Yes, well, so what if I baited him in, however unintentionally," she muttered to herself as the elevator doors closed in front of her. She punched the button to his floor with a shaky finger. "He bloody well took that bait, didn't he?" And isn't that what she wanted him to do? Take her bait?

Dear Lord, yes. Repeatedly. And with great abandon.

She fanned herself and resisted checking her reflection in the mirrored walls. It was one thing to decide to do the femme fatale thing, another altogether to convince her body to play along with the game. She'd just have to hope her neck wasn't as splotchy as it felt.

Her resolve lasted a full ten seconds, then she peeked. One tiny darted glance in the mirror, but it left her blanching. It was even worse than she suspected. The splotches only completed the look. Hair she'd somehow convinced herself looked tousled and sexy back in her hotel room, actually resembled more of a bird's nest. After the windstorm. Her eyes, which she'd taken great pains to line and smudge oh so artistically, didn't at all capture that bedroom-dreamy look she'd been aiming for. More like an insomniac after her fourth straight night of sleeplessness.

Her cheeks were pale, her mouth pinched in at the corners, her lower lip was red and puffy where she'd apparently been gnawing at it like a trapped field mouse.

"You're such a loss," she said, disgusted. "What were you thinking?"

Dulcet tones announced she'd arrived at her chosen floor. She impulsively leaned forward to punch the lobby button as the door slid open.

Too late.

"Sod it," she uttered in miserable disbelief.

Tucker Greywolf, in all his sexy, confident, take-me-now glory, stood not three feet away.

There was a bank of at least eight elevators, with who knew how many guests staying on the thirty-fifth floor…and he had to be standing in front of hers. Right at that moment.

Her finger, frozen on the lobby button, caused the doors to slide shut again, mercifully hiding her from view. Her sigh of trembling relief lasted less than a full second.

A broad, tanned hand jammed itself between the doors at the last possible second, forcing them back open.

"Misty?"

Please Lord have mercy on my vainglorious soul

and swallow me up whole this very instant, she fervently prayed. Adding for good measure that she'd never again try to pretend to be anything other than what she was. A woman meant to live vicariously through the thrills of her fictional characters.

Unfortunately God, in his infinite wisdom, apparently felt she'd learn more from staying right where she was.

There would be no pretending this was a coincidence. Caught at her worst, she simply didn't have the wherewithal to craft the witty repartee required for such a farce. Miss Pottingham would surely demand her graduate certificate be rescinded, effective immediately.

She automatically lifted her hand toward her hair, realized it was a lost cause not worth attempting and let it drop limply to her side again. "Hello."

Tucker pressed the doors completely open and took her by the elbow, tugging her gently from the elevator car. "Are you okay? What's wrong? Has something happened?"

Hysterical laughter was probably not the appropriate response to such a sincere query. But surely he'd share the humor in seeing how totally opposite his reaction was to the one she'd hoped for when she'd planned this rendezvous. Mercifully, or perhaps not depending on how one looked at it, any convulsive gasp of laughter she might have let out died an instant later. The very same instant she realized Tucker was not alone.

There was a gentleman standing just behind him, and judging from the interested look on his face, he wasn't merely another guest waiting for the next available car.

Tucker gently shook her elbow. "Misty?"

She blinked at him. "Oh. No, nothing of the sort." She safely withdrew her elbow from his grasp. His very warm, broad-handed, confident grasp. What a pity she'd never feel those hands on her now. "I'm entirely fine." Which was, quite possibly, the biggest whopper she'd ever told. He apparently thought so, too.

The concern didn't leave his eyes. If anything, it intensified. Or something did. The air between them was alive to the point of being electric.

"Were you coming to see me?"

"I—" She darted a look at the man behind him, then back at him. "You're on your way out. Don't let me hold you up." *Clever avoidance tactic there, Misty.* One her characters employed routinely and which she borrowed without guilt or shame. Anything to end this little reunion as swiftly as possible.

The other man took that moment to step up and extend his hand. "Hi, I'm Ted Strosnyder, with the LVMPD. You must be the author I heard about."

And here she'd thought it impossible to be any more mortified. Apparently Riggins and Faulkner had felt it necessary to tell the entire department they'd interviewed the queen of smut. At least, judging from the look in his eyes, that was how he'd categorized her.

She'd come up against this kind of leering narrow-mindedness before. For that very reason she kept a pithy little arsenal of comebacks, all delivered in her stiffest Miss Pottingham accent. Very effective. However, at the moment, with Tucker standing so near and being all concerned and...so, well, male, her mind went completely blank.

Tucker, sworn to protect and defend, bless his heart, stepped in and saved the day. Or at least the moment.

"Ted, I'm sorry, but it looks like I won't be able to head to the lab with you. I'd completely forgotten our appointment." He sent a look her way, encouraging her to ad lib with him.

"That's quite alright," she said, thankful for the out, but at this point she'd just as soon leave them both to whatever it was they'd been intent on doing. This had been a bad idea all around. She should have stuck to her flight plans. "You two go on. Sounds important."

Ted, grinning like men did when confronted with a woman who'd made a career out of hot sex, even if it was just writing about it, shook his head. "Why don't you join us? I'll give you a tour of the facility." He tried to move in, take her arm, but Tucker neatly maneuvered her to his other side, away from Ted's grasp, and pressed the button for the elevator.

"You have business," she said, appreciative of Tucker's attempts, but shifting away from both of them. "I'll just be on my way."

"Nonsense," Ted insisted. "Come on, you never know when you might need something like this in one of your books. 'Lust in the Lab' or something equally kinky." He chuckled, vastly amused by himself. "What do you say?"

She glanced up at Tucker who sent her an apologetic shrug, but said nothing. *Gee, thanks,* she silently messaged back. For which she was rewarded with a wicked grin.

I know what I want.

His words wouldn't stop echoing in her mind. That smile didn't help matters any. And apparently, right now, he wanted her to go with them.

The elevator door opened right then and he pressed that wide, warm palm between her shoulder blades and gently steered her into the empty car. Then, once they'd turned their backs to the rear wall, he slowly drew one blunt-tipped finger down her spine, letting his hand drift away just as he reached the swell of her bottom.

Her thighs trembled and she was pretty sure her panties were on their way to being soaked.

Okay, so just maybe her plan wasn't *that* horrid after all.

When they stepped out into the lobby, both men looked at her expectantly. She suddenly wished she'd taken Tucker up on his willingness to forgo his plans for her. But it was too late for that. "I'd be interested in seeing the lab." Not a total lie. But she was far more interested in seeing Tucker's equipment than that of the local police department. "If you're sure I won't be in the way."

"Nonsense," Ted assured her again. He stepped in to direct her across the lobby, but once again Tucker stepped smoothly in and made it clear, with one look, that Ted could leer and drool all he wanted, but his hands were to be kept to himself.

For that alone Misty could have kissed him. And she planned to find a way to do just that as soon as they were alone. She wasn't used to having anyone run interference for her, had grown used to providing her own defense. It felt rather nice, knowing he was looking out for her.

Tucker's hand brushed softly along her lower back before settling there as he guided her out the glass doors to the curbside. She shivered at his touch. Okay, so she planned to do a whole lot more than deliver a thank-you kiss. One glance up into his amused black eyes told her they were about to have the fastest tour of the lab as was humanly possible.

She should have felt guilty about that. About interfering. Then Tucker climbed in the back of the cab and scooted over to leave room for Ted. Which meant pressing the length of his thigh along the length of hers. Suddenly she didn't feel the least bit guilty. A girl did what a girl had to do. Certainly a Misty Fortune girl, anyway.

She kept her gaze out the window while Ted prattled on about all the latest forensic tools his team had acquired. She assumed it was for Tucker's benefit, but another glance in Tucker's direction led to the discovery that his attention was very exclusively focused on her.

She flashed to that moment in the hall, when he'd trapped her body between his and the wall. About the very intent promise he'd made her. Well, those promises were still alive and well and beaming down at her in a way that was impossible to misinterpret.

Ted's babble faded into the background, forgotten,

and she let herself sink into the promises being made in those eyes. He lifted one eyebrow in a silent question. She knew what he was asking. Had she come back to take him up on his offer?

With the slightest dip of her chin, she gave him her answer. Then did her best to resist the urge to scratch at her neck when he grinned and mouthed, "Thank you."

TUCKER SHIFTED as best he could in cramped conditions, hoping beyond hope the cramped condition in his pants would subside shortly. Had it not been for Ted—who he was rapidly wishing he'd never met—he might have taken her right there in the back of the cab. In fact, even Ted's presence might not have stopped him, as he'd forgotten all about the man the moment he'd locked eyes with Misty.

But a moment later the cab pulled to the curb and they were out and heading into LVMPD's forensic lab. Had he been any less painfully aroused, he'd have laughed at the irony of finally getting inside a place he'd always wanted to see…and wishing he were inside something else entirely.

Ted led them into a small conference room and Tucker shook hands with Mig and Patterson. "Thanks for letting me come check out your toy box."

"We're hoping you'll like it well enough to want to stick around."

Tucker just smiled. Then Ted was ushering Misty forward. "Ms. Smythe-Davies—"

"Please, Misty is fine."

Tucker could see from Ted's oozing smile that he

thought she was just fine, too. He shot Mig a look and the detective gave him a brief, apologetic shrug. Apparently what Ted knew about forensics made up for what he didn't know about women, which was next to nothing if his behavior was any indication.

Tucker kept his hands at his sides, but his attention remained on high alert. He wondered if she always had to put up with guys like him. Then he swallowed a smirk of his own. Right now, the thoughts going through his mind didn't exactly separate him from the wolf pack.

"This is Miguez and Patterson, two of our pre-eminent forensic's specialists," Ted introduced.

Mig laughed. "Right. He only sweet-talks us when he wants something."

Just then another man entered the room. He was young, distracted, wearing a white lab coat with goggles shoved up on his head. His name tag read Dennis the Menace.

"Hey, Menace," Patterson said. "What you got for us?"

"A match," he said, holding up two computer printouts. "The fiber you found inside the wound matches the sportcoat fiber from the husband."

Mig held up his hand and Patterson reluctantly slapped it. "Right again, my man," Mig crowed. "It's always the husband."

Dennis cleared his throat. "Actually, the percentage of spousal conviction in cases like this is—"

"Yeah, yeah," Mig interrupted, "let a guy have his moment, will ya?"

Everyone chuckled, except for Dennis, who said,

"I've still got two other tests to run, but I thought you'd want to know this."

"Thanks, man. Appreciate it."

Dennis nodded and headed back out, clearly more comfortable with his microscopes and slides than he was socializing.

Mig pulled out a phone and made a quick call. "Yeah," he said when someone answered, "pull the husband in. We got a match." He spoke for another few moments, then clicked off. He sat down and flipped open a file folder, then motioned everyone else to sit down.

Tucker slid smoothly in front of Ted and pulled out an end chair for Misty, then planted himself next to her. He expected a brief smile of thanks for his rescue, but she was glancing at the pictures that slid from the file.

Mig hurriedly scooped them back up. "You don't want to look at these."

Misty merely smiled and shifted back in her seat. "Actually, despite the misfortune suffered by Ms. Denton, I'm rather fascinated by the whole thing. But I don't want to get in the way."

"You aren't," Ted assured her, a little too enthusiastically for Tucker's taste. "As soon as we're done here, I'll give you that tour I promised." He turned away, then quickly looked back at Tucker. "You, too, of course."

"Of course," Tucker replied mildly. Mig glanced up at him, then at Ted, smiled and shook his head lightly as he looked back down at his notes. "While we haven't entirely ruled out the Blackstone employee who was, uh, servicing Ms. Denton at or around the time of death, we can now establish that Drew Ralston was in the room with her.''

''The jacket fiber was actually in the gunshot wound?''

Mig looked at Tucker. ''Yes. She was shot point-blank. Apparently he was holding her at the time. After we found the fiber, we got a warrant, searched the house and found the jacket in the trash out back. Bullet hole in the right lower front pocket. Apparently he had the gun in his pocket, pulled her tight against him, maybe during a struggle, and shot her.''

''Any marks to indicate a fight?''

Mig shook his head. ''Just the single gunshot wound.''

''Was Ralston interviewed last night with the rest of the guests?'' Tucker asked.

Ted spoke. ''He wasn't on the premises when we arrived. We sent a car to their home address, to inform him of what happened, ask some questions. He claimed to be home all night, but we already have a witness—a Blackstone driver—who claims he saw Ralston getting out of a cab at the resort gates within the time frame of the time of death. Once we got the warrant this morning, he lawyered up. But we have enough for an indictment now, so it doesn't matter. He won't talk to us, but he'll have to talk to the judge.''

''So, what do you need me for?'' Tucker asked.

Mig grinned. ''Well, there was some concern initially with the splatter formation, trying to judge the height of the shooter, but now that we have this...

What can I say? Dead bodies tell many tales, and this particular tale—'' he held up the computer printouts ''—is going to put Mr. Drew Ralston in jail.''

"So, Ms. Denton lives here in Vegas, but was staying at Blackstone's?" Mig turned to Misty when she spoke. She smiled. "I'm sorry, I don't mean to interrupt, it's just that, as a writer...well, I'm curious. I hope you don't mind."

Mig smiled. "That's okay. She was apparently invited by Mr. Blackstone for their grand opening in January," he said, "but wasn't able to schedule a stay here until now. Seems Blackstone had to do a little convincing."

Tucker noticed a tinge of pink grace her cheeks, and her hand fluttered to her neck. Apparently Patsy Denton wasn't the only celebrity invited, or the only one needing some convincing. He wondered what Blackstone had had to offer to get her to agree to come.

"So she didn't choose to come here, then?" Misty asked. "She was just here as a favor? But you said she was, um, taking advantage of the resort services..." She trailed off as all of the men looked up at her.

Tucker realized they were all thinking—and quite graphically—that she'd been there for the same purpose.

"They have couple's packages here, don't they," Tucker said, drawing their attention to him. "Perhaps they came together, only Mr. Ralston wasn't able to arrive until later."

Patterson shook his head. "No, she was signed up

for the—'' He pulled the file around so he could read it. ''Cleopatra. This is where she gets to command a bunch of guys to—''

Tucker cleared his throat and Patterson broke off and coughed. ''Sorry, ma'am.''

Misty smiled. ''It's okay. I'm…somewhat familiar with that type of thing.''

Tucker had to hide his smile as all three men found somewhere else to look for a moment. He admired the way she handled the attention, directly, but with just enough cool aplomb to discourage further comment. He imagined she'd had a lot of practice at it. But it didn't stop him from wondering what *her* package plan had been….

''So,'' Mig said, pausing to sip his coffee. ''Jealousy seems to be the prime possibility for motive. He's got plenty of his own money, so I doubt this was planned for some inheritance or insurance deal. Classic crime of passion. With the matching fiber to put him on the scene, I'm sure it's only a matter of time before we nail his ass—er, hide, to the wall.''

''Well, he knew what type of resort this was, and what she was here for,'' Ted added, ''so there was some premeditation to it. He could do some serious time.''

''Who were the other suspects?''

The four men looked at Misty once again. ''Excuse me?'' Mig asked.

''You said there were other suspects. One was the employee who was with her. I'm just curious, who was the other one?''

''Actually, there were several employees assigned

to Ms. Denton, but only one had gone in at the time of death. He claimed she was dead when he arrived and he was the one who alerted the staff, who called it in.''

"So, then he was telling the truth," Misty said.

Mig and Patterson both shrugged. "We don't know that for sure, but it doesn't look like he pulled the trigger.''

"So then it's not a crime of passion. She wasn't in the act.'' This came from Tucker.

"She was here, she was, shall we say, prepared and waiting for the evening's festivities to begin. I don't think the district attorney is going to worry if the guy wasn't actually there in the room with her yet. There was no doubt what she was in that room to do.'' He looked at Misty. "But, as a matter of procedure, we always take a close look at whoever discovers the body.'' He shrugged. "You never know, so you never rule anything out until the evidence is all in.''

She nodded, chewing a bit on her bottom lip.

Tucker had noticed her doing that the night before, as she'd talked to the detectives. It made him want to do unnatural things to her mouth. He forced himself to look away as his body responded yet again to the visuals that seemed to just spring forth every time he looked at her.

Spring forth. There was an apt description of the effect she had on him. And every other male, if the other three men at the table were any indication. *You're as big a hormone-induced jackass as they are, Greywolf, thinking you could make time with her be-*

cause you happened to catch her when her defenses were down.

Though, come to think of it, she hadn't seemed all that defenseless. In fact, she'd been amazingly poised, all things considered. Anyone else put in the potentially mortifying position she'd been put in would not have been able to pull it together so smoothly. She'd chatted up the detectives as if they'd been having tea in her salon. As if she'd been fully dressed and not wearing that filmy piece of nothing.

A piece of nothing he remembered quite clearly as he'd been up against it in that hallway when he'd so badly wanted to take that mouth of hers and—

"Greywolf?"

His attention jerked back by Mig's voice, he had to backpedal quickly and hope like hell he hadn't been leering or worse, drooling. *Really, you need to get a grip.*

What he needed was to get Misty out of here and alone. With him. Until he'd exhausted every one of the scenarios that kept playing out in his mind.

"I'm sorry, I was thinking about the case. About how Ralston got on the grounds. Do cabs routinely let people off at the end of the drive?"

Mig ducked his gaze, but not before Tucker saw his smile. Still, he rescued him before Ted could make some smarmy-ass comment and ruin any chance he had to not be lumped in with the usual men who couldn't stop thinking about what she did for a living.

"No. In fact, cabs aren't allowed on Blackstone grounds. Only their own drivers can get past the front gate. Which also confirms that he wasn't here to join in the fun and games with his wife. Otherwise she could have had a car sent for him.''

''Mmm,'' Tucker said, sending a silent thanks to Mig for covering his ass. He'd owe him one. ''Good point.''

Not that he needed to worry. Misty wasn't paying any attention to him anyway. She propped her elbows on the table. ''So, who was the third suspect?''

''We don't know,'' Patterson piped in. ''All we know is there was another woman in her room that night.''

''Her Blackstone assistant maybe?''

Patterson and Mig shook their heads. ''Not unless she was sharing a glass of wine with her.''

''Which is against company policy,'' Ted injected.

''There were two wineglasses with two different shades of lipstick on the glass. One had been wiped off, but we found the napkin in the trash, and lifted traces of it off the glass as well. No usable prints, though, but we're running tests to see if both colors belonged to Ms. Denton.''

''You think she changed lipstick and drank from a second glass?'' Tucker asked.

Mig shrugged. ''No, but again, we don't leave anything unexamined. It could have been someone who came by earlier in the day and had nothing to do with this. But the fact that the attempt was made to wipe it clean makes it stand out as potential evidence.''

''Even if it was her lipstick, couldn't someone else have borrowed it?'' Misty asked.

''Sure. Unlikely, but sure. I'm guessing it won't match the lipsticks we took from her room or purse.

I'm almost positive there was someone else in that room.''

"No other evidence?'' Tucker asked. "No chance another guest stopped by?''

"Not that anyone's admitting. She had no scheduled guests either. Still, we'd like to track down whoever the second set of lip prints belonged to. Possible witness to the murder, or to the motive.''

"Could she have come in with Mr. Ralston?'' Misty asked. "Maybe he had someone else on the side himself and this *was* premeditated. Maybe it wasn't about money, or jealousy, but about love.''

Mig grinned. "You know, you might have missed your calling. You do any suspense novels?''

Misty's eyes did that twinkle thing. "Sometimes the greatest suspense in a person's life is falling in love. Or it should be.'' She shrugged, but smiled as she shaded her neck with her hands.

Tucker was becoming more and more enamored of those little splotches by the moment. Maybe because they appeared to be the only chink in her otherwise impeccably British armor.

"Reading people, seeing beneath the surface,'' Mig shrugged. "That's not always easy, but you have to get inside their head. Not everyone can do that.''

"Well, I don't know Drew Ralston, have never met him, so I can't really say if my idea is even close to the mark. As for understanding motivation, well, that's my job. In fact, often I do a sort of interrogation of my own characters, to learn more about them. Helps to flesh them out, make them more real.''

"Why bother to flesh them out?'' Ted asked with

a self-amused grin. "As long as they're in the flesh most of the time, right?" He looked around as if expecting everyone else to laugh with him. When Mig and Patterson just rolled their eyes, Tucker moved to intercept, but Misty beat him to it.

"Have you ever read one of my books, Mr. Strosnyder?"

Tucker hid a smile. The regal queen's English had made a return appearance. Why he thought she'd needed defending he had no idea.

"Actually, I haven't had the pleasure." He'd obviously meant that last part as a pun, but even he wasn't foolish enough to look for support this time.

"Well, I think you might be surprised by the depth and complexity of my plotting." She leaned forward, bestowing on him her best smile. "I don't ever underestimate the intelligence of my readers, or my characters. I think a believable and enjoyable story is only truly entertaining when an author can seduce her reader's mind, don't you?"

"Uh, yeah." Ted's face had become a bit flushed. "I guess so."

Misty pushed her chair back and stood with a smile. "I appreciate you allowing me to sit in on your discussion, gentlemen. Be assured I won't speak of it to anyone. And as much as I'd have enjoyed the tour, I'm afraid I have a flight to catch."

She's leaving? Today? Tucker stood abruptly. She'd agreed to four days. Hadn't she? What else had that little chin dip in the taxi meant?

By the time he gathered his wits, she was already shaking hands with everyone and heading to the door.

"Wait." He couldn't just let her walk away. Not again. "I'll see you out, get you a cab."

She smiled at him, the same serene curve of her lips she'd been giving the others during the entire meeting. But this time it didn't reach her eyes. There was some other message there, but he was damned if he knew what it was. "I'm sure I can manage."

"I insist." Tucker ignored the speculative looks of everyone still seated at the table.

She merely lifted her shoulder in a half shrug and stepped into the hall.

Tucker turned to the other men. "I'm sorry."

Mig and Patterson both grinned. "Oh no, we perfectly understand," Patterson offered.

"Mighty chivalrous of you," Mig added.

"Sure we can't interest you in the tour?" This from Ted.

Both Mig and Patterson just gave him a look. Ted merely shrugged as if he didn't understand his offense.

Tucker shook his hand. "Some other time, maybe."

Then he let himself out and found Misty waiting for him, that ambiguous expression still on her face.

"What time is your flight?" he asked.

She studied him for a long moment, then seemed to come to some kind of decision. Tucker felt his heart stop in the space of time it took her to finally answer.

"I don't know," she said, "I haven't actually booked it yet."

6
_____

THERE, SHE'D SAID IT. More or less, anyway. It was what she'd tracked him down for, after all. Of course, she hadn't planned on announcing her availability in the hallway of a police lab facility, but then nothing between them had been remotely typical up to this point. Why start being predictable now?

The slow grin that crossed his face did wonders for her confidence…and her pulse rate. Dear Lord, she felt another lapse of decorum coming on. A small smile of her own threatened to surface. *About time.*

"Would you like to grab something to eat?" he asked. "Discuss…flight plans?"

Did she want to get to know him better first? Or would it be best to, well, fling herself into this fling? After all, she wasn't planning on anything long term here. "I have a suite at the Bellagio. We could…order in."

If she wasn't so nervous, she'd laugh at herself. After all her talk in the conference room, here she was, acting out Ted Strosnyder's most prurient fantasies. Only she was acting them out with Tucker. Which made it entirely different, of course.

He didn't leer at her…or worse, condescend to her. In fact he hadn't made mention of her occupation at all, or the fact that when they'd met she'd been naked and oiled and ready for God knew what.

"I was thinking maybe something outdoors," he said.

Her eyes widened in surprise.

His danced. "For lunch. We can discuss what comes next while we eat."

In her books, men never said no when a lady proposed sex. And there was no doubt he knew she'd been offering herself for lunch.

The man who had trapped her against the wall last night wouldn't have wanted to waste time with the midday meal. Unless that meal was her. She subdued her urge to shudder with visualized pleasure. Had he changed his mind? Or maybe her set down of Mr. Strosnyder had him thinking he had to woo her into bed.

If he only knew.

She started down the hall, away from potential prying eyes and ears. "Lunch would be lovely," she said, then slowed and turned, catching his gaze with hers. If she was going to do this, she bloody well wasn't going to mince around. "But unnecessary."

Tucker gave her a look, but said nothing, pausing only long enough to ask the receptionist to put a call in for a cab. Then he held the door open for her. As she passed by him, he dipped his head and said, "I want to watch you eat."

There was no subduing the shiver that raced through her this time. So, the man was a sensualist. She wasn't surprised.

"And besides," he added with a boyish grin, "I'm hungry."

That surprised a laugh from her and propelled her out the door. She couldn't peg him, he wasn't easily categorized, much less predictable. She liked that. And since she didn't know what to say to a man she'd just offered herself to, she watched the road for the taxi.

He stepped in behind her. "I'll have a better chance of finishing my meal if we eat out." She stilled at his nearness. He waited until she shifted her head slightly so she could see him from the corner of her eye. "And I'd rather satisfy one hunger, before embarking on satisfying another."

She tried desperately to maintain a serene outward expression. Which was a challenge, as chaos reigned within her. The things this man said to her!

"You handled yourself well in there," he said, stepping away.

She faced him, surprised at the shift in topic. Indefinable, unpredictable.

"With Strosnyder," he clarified. "And with the rest of it. Your take on the case was interesting. But I meant Strosnyder. I imagine you get that a lot."

"Not often, really. But then I don't make a habit of sharing the details of my occupation with just anyone." She smiled. "Cocktail party chitchat is far simpler that way."

"Not as interesting though."

"Depends on your point of view."

He just smiled.

The cab pulled up then and he held the door for

her before sliding into the back seat. "Any recommendations on a good place to eat al fresco," he asked the cabbie as they settled in. When the man just looked at him, Tucker said, "A place that has tables outside, for lunch?"

The man's face lit up. "No problem," he said, the words heavily accented. He pulled away from the curb and Tucker turned his attention back to Misty.

"You're just going to trust his selection?" Misty asked.

"Why not? He knows the city better than I do. Unless you have a place in mind?"

"I believe I mentioned the place I had in mind."

That lifted his eyebrows a twitch, she noted. She shifted her gaze out the window, hiding her pleasure at being the one to do the surprising. She vowed to do more of it.

"So you did. Well, why don't we just consider lunch the first stop on our adventure?"

She thought about what he'd told her the night before. "I can't promise you the entire four days."

He picked up her hand, turned it over and traced his thumb over her palm, then down each finger. It caused the most delicious sensation to curl in the pit of her stomach.

"Why don't we just begin with lunch, see where that leads us? Whenever you decide it's time to leave, you can book your flight home." He traced his fingertips to her wrist, across her stuttering pulse. "I don't see any reason to set boundaries on this, do you?"

She thought she could drown in those dark eyes of

his. Eyes that promised nothing…and everything. No boundaries. "No, no I don't." She tried to get her thoughts on track, but all of her attention was focused on his hand, touching hers. His skin was darker, his Native American heritage a definite opposite to her English one. And where she was pale all over…she imagined he wasn't. His hands were big, and strong…and very possibly he was going to be putting them on her in places that… Well, that delicious sensation curled a bit lower as her imagination took over.

"What—what about your seminars?" Her throat was dry and a bit tight. Perhaps that was an appropriate reaction when one was about to embark on a sexual liaison with a stranger. An entirely different sort of stranger than the professionals she'd come seeking. She looked down at their joined hands and couldn't seem to summon up any moral outrage over her decision. Impatience, that was the uppermost feeling she was having at the moment. "I'd hate to think I was taking you away from your classes."

"Some of the most important things I've learned have come from just doing them." He flashed that grin at her. The grin that told her he'd learned quite a few things in a "hands-on" fashion.

And right now all she wanted was those hands on her.

"No better teacher than experience," she murmured in agreement. It was why she'd come here, after all. She'd read the books. Hell, she'd written some. And the only thing that had made her an expert was in knowing what she wanted. And what she wanted done to her. But turning that into a reality?

He pulled her hand up to his mouth just then, and kissed her palm, just a warm press of his lips, then he drifted those lips to the inside of her wrist, and kissed her there as well. She almost swallowed her tongue.

"Your turn," he said, lowering their still-joined hands.

"What?" she choked out.

"That's how this works, right? I try something, then you try something? How else are we going to discover what we like?"

"Right," she said, suddenly unsteady. Her turn. "Okay then." She supposed she could simply mirror his actions, kiss his palm.

But this wasn't just about pleasing him, it was also about learning what she was capable of. She didn't want to copy him. She wanted to do things, try things she'd never tried before, things she'd only written about. So. What would she honestly like to do to him right now? That could be done in the back of a taxi, that is.

She shifted closer to him, then a bit closer still, until she was pressed up against him from shoulder to thigh. He watched her, but said nothing, made no move to anticipate what she was about to do. With her free hand, she reached up and softly stroked the side of his face.

His eyes flared, but he remained still. "Soft skin," she murmured, "for such a hard face." His jaw and cheekbones were prominent. "Close shave," she went on, rubbing her fingertips gently across his chin.

"I rarely have to. Blessing of my ancestors," he

said, barely moving his lips. And what lips they were, looking almost carved from the smooth planes of his cheeks and jaw…and yet that bottom lip held just a hint of fullness in the middle, a hint of seduction….

Her breath grew the slightest bit ragged, but she continued her exploration. "Who are your ancestors?" She traced her fingers across his other cheek and along the dark slash of his eyebrows. Thick lashes framed dark, exotic eyes.

"Apache," he said, his voice a bit tense, his jaw flexed.

She glanced into those eyes, so black. Even this close up it was hard to determine where iris ended and pupil began. "So fierce," she said softly, then finally drew her fingertips to his mouth, running them along his lips, so chiseled, so seductive.

"So hard," he corrected, then turned his face from her still-questing fingers.

She let her hand drop away, but couldn't help the smile. "Still interested in lunch?"

He shot her a direct look that made her pulse skyrocket. "My hunger is building by the minute."

Christ but the man made her wet. "Then why—"

The taxi pulled to the curb just then. "We are here," the cabbie announced.

Tucker looked out the window at the small café. "So we are." He opened the door and all the tension that had mounted between them slid out with him. He kept possession of her hand as he helped her out.

"Wait, let me take care of the meter," she said.

"I'll take care of it."

She would have argued with him, but she was already on the sidewalk. She wasn't looking to be taken care of. At least not in that manner. When the cab pulled away and Tucker turned back to her, she got right to it. "I am perfectly capable of—"

Tucker palmed her hips and tugged her forward until her body came flush up against his. There was no mistaking how aroused he was. "I'm perfectly aware of your capabilities. Remind me not to play games with you while using public transportation."

"Oh," she said, unable to respond more clearly, because her body was busy doing all the responding at the moment. She went to step back, but his arm slid around her back, keeping her right where she was.

"Come here," he said, moving them away from the entrance to the café. He let go of her then, shot her that boyish grin when she gave him a questioning look. "I need to not touch you for a couple of minutes. Let things settle down."

Smiling, Misty decided she rather liked this femme fatale stuff. Perhaps she should have tried it sooner. And maybe she would have if she'd met the right man. The ones she'd dated, behavior like this would have seemed silly, forced. With Tucker…well, it was all she could do not to whistle for anther taxi and drag him back to her room.

However, she was beginning to see the attraction of drawing things out a bit. Who knew foreplay could begin so far outside the bedroom? Well, she did, of course. In fiction, anyway.

"What's going on behind that very wicked smile?" he asked.

"Wicked is it?" Her smile grew. "Well, perhaps

that's apt, as that's how I'm feeling at the moment. Can I share something with you?"

"I'm rather hoping you'll share a lot with me," he said, his attempt at her accent so laughable it was cute.

She merely gave him a look, then said, "Despite the manner in which we met, and despite my occupation as well, this sort of thing isn't my...shall we say, forte."

"I'd never have guessed."

Her eyebrows lifted. "What is that supposed to mean?"

He gestured for her to go ahead of him into the café and didn't answer until they were seated at a small glass-and-wrought iron table placed at the outside corner of the eating area.

He took her hand again, over the table, and toyed with her fingers. She decided she didn't care what he meant, as long as he kept touching her.

"You have this interesting duality," he said.

"Duality? Now there's a word."

He shrugged. "It was the best I could come up with, but it fits."

Intrigued, she asked, "What are these dual attributes then?"

"On the one hand, you are a woman who writes of the intricacies of passion between men and women." He smiled. "It is heterosexual fiction, right?"

She laughed. "You would be correct."

"Okay. And then there is the manner in which we first met. And I will admit to being very curious about why you were there, whether it was personal or just professional research.'' He traced his fingers along hers. ''But all that is the writer you, the professional you. The you that put Ted so perfectly in his place. You're absolutely confident about what and who you are as a writer.''

''You got all that from a brief conversation at a police lab?''

''No, I mostly got that from the way you conducted your own interrogation of Faulkner and Riggins.''

''Ah. I'd forgotten you eavesdropped on that.''

He just smiled. ''I am an investigator.''

She slowly withdrew her fingers from his. ''And the other part of me? I suppose that would be the obvious novice in the actual practicing of those intricacies you spoke of earlier. Was I so transparent then?''

''No, not at all. In fact, I don't think I've ever been so turned on by a woman touching my face.'' He let that sink in for a moment, then said, ''What I meant was that you project a certain 'hands-off' attitude. Maybe it's that British stiff upper lip thing. Or maybe you just have to put up that wall, for the very reason that what you write possibly encourages men to assume a familiarity you don't appreciate. You never once gave the impression that you made a habit of devouring whatever man caught your eye. But I never doubted you could.''

She had no idea what to say to that.

''You intrigued me,'' he went on. ''Fascinated me, as I told you when we met. In fact, I can honestly say no woman has ever caught my attention as squarely as you did."

She smiled then, surprised at how easy it was to relax with him, especially considering the extremely personal nature of their conversation. "I daresay meeting a woman when she is fully naked and posed on a bed of silk pillows might warrant a bit of attention."

"Perhaps," he conceded easily. "But it was watching you with the detectives that really worked me up."

She was saved from immediately responding when the waiter approached with their menus. He recited the specials and they both ordered quickly, almost obliviously it seemed to Misty. Right now the menu they were most interested in perusing wasn't the one with food listed on it. Once the young man had walked away, Misty turned her attention back to Tucker. "I will tell you why I came to Blackstone's, but first it's my turn for confession."

Tucker lifted his hands. "Tell me everything."

Her lips curved and she paused. "I'm not so sure I should. Confidence is something I don't think you ever lack."

"You'd be surprised."

"How so?"

"When you went back into the office last night, to contact your director, I was honestly torn on whether or not to follow you."

"Which you didn't. Were you honestly afraid of rejection?"

He shook his head. "Not afraid. Although I'll admit, I'm not usually in the position where I have to chase. At least, not with any great effort anyway.''

"Really," she parroted, "I never would have guessed."

His grin was tempered with a self-deprecating laugh. "The town I'm from isn't all that big, so—"

She waved a hand. "I'm quite sure that wouldn't matter. So, you didn't follow me because I wounded your ego when I didn't immediately fall at your feet, begging you for a wild, four-day fling?"

"Not at all, although I admit to extreme disappointment. But I didn't follow you because, if I had, you'd have turned me down flat."

"What makes you so sure?"

"I came on pretty strong, our initial meeting not being what you'd call remotely typical, and you'd just been through an interrogation by police investigating a homicide." His grin surfaced again, only this time that shade of cockiness had returned. "I'm somewhat self-aware when it comes to what kind of effect I have on a woman, but there are things even I can't overcome."

She had to laugh. He was truly incorrigible. "I'm surprised the women of your hometown ever let you leave it."

"They're not so impressed with me. Most of them have known me all my life."

She'd bet the women back home were plenty impressed. For all his attitude and assuredness, he was quite gentlemanly and cordial. It was a power punch combo.

"Is that why not one of them has managed to snag you?"

He laughed. "I've known most of them all their lives, too. After so many years, that kind of history has a way of rendering them all family of sorts."

Yeah, she'd just bet that's how they saw him. Like a brother. She managed to refrain from a rather unladylike snort.

"I could ask the same of you. A big city like New York, filled with men from all over the world. Money, power, polish. And yet you remain unsnagged as well."

She conceded his point. "Not because of any familial feelings, I assure you. It simply hasn't happened." She didn't want to talk about her dismal track record with men, although boring would be a better term. She was anything but bored at the moment. In fact, she couldn't ever remember feeling so entirely engaged. And they were just eating lunch. She couldn't imagine what this intensity would feel like in bed. "So," she said, pausing to take a sip of her water, cool down her suddenly heated...everything. "You were just going to let me walk away then? What if I hadn't come to your hotel today? Easy come, easy go?"

"I thought I could let you walk away," he said, suddenly serious. "I'm here to learn and this murder investigation is an opportunity like no other."

"Back to learning by doing."

"Exactly." He pierced her with that black gaze of his. "Except, when I went back to my hotel last night, the only thing on my mind was you. I called Blackstone's first thing this morning, prepared to do whatever I had to, to get you to have lunch with me today. Only you'd already checked out.''

Misty laughed. It was that or fan herself, his attention was so hotly focused on her. ''I certainly feel better about showing up unannounced at your hotel, then.''

''And yet, when I gave us an out to not go with Ted, you didn't pick up on it. I know you understood what I was trying to do. Why back down?''

''I was already having second thoughts in the elevator. As I said earlier, I'm not in the habit of baldly pursuing a man I find attractive. In fact, the more I thought about it, the more nervous I became. I second-guessed everything from my hair to my clothes and was stabbing the lobby button as the doors opened. In fact,'' she laughed wryly, tugging her hand from his to cover her neck, ''I'm getting splotchy again just talking about it. Cursed English skin.''

He leaned over, tugged her hand away. ''I'm very attracted to your English skin. The rest just makes you human. You're already intimidating enough, being perfect would simply be too much.''

She laughed more honestly. ''Outrageous flattery will get you everywhere.''

''Not so outrageous as you think, but I'll keep that in mind.'' He toyed with her hand again. ''You were ready to leave the lab without me, too. Why didn't you?''

She smiled. ''You mean besides the fact that you pursued me out into the hall? Well, that actually brings us back to why I came to Vegas in the first place.''

''To Blackstone's.''

She nodded, then paused, wanting to explain this clearly, but not so that he'd think she was some sort of sexual charity case. ''I'm not inexperienced.''

''I never believed you were.'' He held up a hand. ''And so there is no confusion, I say that in a flattering, you-knock-my-socks-off kind of way.''

She laughed again, amazed at how easy this was when it should be so incredibly awkward. ''Well done,'' she told him.

He merely nodded in an ''I try'' sort of manner, and gestured for her to continue.

''Okay then, we've covered the fact that I don't fling myself at men, but that I have been flung, so to speak. However, there are certain things that I've yearned to do…'' She trailed off, then realizing that, for heaven's sake, she'd come this far, she might as well meet the rest head-on. So she held his gaze squarely and said, ''And there are things I've yearned to have done to me. Yet, I've never managed to meet the man who I felt comfortable enough with to pursue those wants.''

''And that's where Blackstone's came into play?''

''Yes. I came here for me. As a woman, but also as a writer,'' she explained. ''A writer who must rely on a vivid imagination to put together all aspects of her stories. Not just the sexual, mind you. But, I've been at this for some time, and the well, as they say, is running a bit dry.'' She smiled then, mostly at herself. "Both personally and professionally, as it were."

"I love it when you get nervous."

"Am I stammering?" She touched her neck. "Splotchy?"

"Neither. But your accent goes from a casual sort of thing, to this amazingly polished yet edgy kind of tone. Frankly, it turns me on."

She studied him, surprised by his observation. "I suppose I'll have to remember that. For later."

Now he laughed. "Please do." He took her hand in his and pulled her forward until they were both leaning across the table. "Can I interrupt and tell you how glad I am you decided to stay?"

She grinned, feeling ever so much the same way. "Why yes, yes you may."

"And can I also tell you that I'm flattered and at the same time a bit nervous."

Now she sat back. "You? What on earth do you have to be nervous about?"

"Well, you've checked out of Blackstone's, your quest unfulfilled. But you've opted to stay...and sought me out instead. I can only conclude that the things you wanted to explore at Blackstone's, you're hoping to explore, at least to some extent, with me."

She supposed she should be embarrassed to have her desires put in such bald terms. But she'd already come to the conclusion that he was her best bet if she was to indeed do some carnal exploring. "You seemed willing enough to take on an adventure."

"Yes, but then I wasn't aware of your agenda."

"I don't have an agenda."

"What exactly was it you'd signed up for at Blackstone's?"

Now it was her turn to tease and she enjoyed that it came so naturally. With him. "You've been dying to learn that little tidbit since you found me in that room, haven't you?"

He shrugged, unrepentant. "I am human."

"And an investigator. You didn't ferret out that little bit of information with your innumerable skills?"

"I don't know how innumerable they are," he responded with a wolfish grin, "but no, I'd never pry into your privacy like that."

And she knew he was absolutely sincere. "I detect a bit of shining armor there."

Now he laughed. "Oh, there's nothing noble about the fun I had imagining what package you signed up for, trust me."

"I'm intrigued. What did you think I chose?"

"I never saw the brochure. I came up with my own."

"Did you now. And I suppose, given your earlier comments, they had something to do with me ordering about my royal subjects."

Now his expression turned downright wicked. It gave her the most delicious sensation between her tightly clenched thighs.

"Actually, you said something a bit…revealing, when we first met."

"Did I?" She wracked her brain, but it had been such a momentarily mortifying situation, she had no idea what all she'd said. "What did I reveal?"

"Well, let's just say I don't believe you wanted to be the one doing the ordering."

Now she knew she was splotchy. He simply grinned knowingly and leaned back in his seat.

When she refused to respond—after all, what could she have said?—he said, "Brochure packages aside, you must have compiled a list of sorts, of things you wanted to experience."

She lifted one eyebrow, drawing on every skill Miss Pottingham ever expounded on, and said, quite stiffly, "You're willing to do the entire list then? How noble of you."

He paled, for just a split second, but it was enough to make her burst out laughing. "Honestly, Tucker, when I walked away from Blackstone's I'd pretty much given up on my quest, as you called it. I wasn't entirely comfortable with doing things that way, anyway. I just thought that was my only chance."

"So...why are we here?"

"Because you offered me an adventure. A real one, not one for hire. If I happen to learn a few things on the way..." She shrugged, then allowed a wicked smile of her own to surface as she picked up his hand. She turned it palm up and traced her fingers across the warm expanse of skin. "Well, let's just say I'm fairly certain you could teach me a few things. And I mean that in a flattering you-make-my-knickers-wet kind of way."

He'd just picked up his water. Her casually spoken words had him choking on his first sip.

She laughed. Maybe that's why he was so perfect.

Because he wasn't at all perfect. He was just right. "Are you still game?"

He flipped her hand over and trapped it neatly on the table beneath his. All she could think about was having him trap her body just as neatly.

"You only have four days?"

Now it was her turn to choke a little.

He gave her a considering look, then grinned. "If we're focused, we might be able to squeeze it all in by then."

The waiter brought their food to the table then and he released her hand and picked up his fork. "Just so I understand the rules here—"

"There are no rules," she said, shakily picking up her own silverware.

"Perfect. Then I get to do some exploring of my own as well? I have a few of my own little forbidden fantasies."

"Okay, one rule," she clarified, trying not to gulp…or imagine just what kind of fantasies he considered forbidden.

He just smiled. "Only one?"

She just gave him a look. "We have to both be willing or we find something else to try."

"I think I can handle that."

7

FOREPLAY OVER SALAD. What in the hell had he been thinking? He could be in a suite at the Bellagio right this very second. Naked, buried deep inside the woman sitting across from him. Instead he was eating arugula.

"Will you be caring for any dessert?"

Tucker looked up at the waiter and had to restrain himself from saying, "Yeah, her."

"None for me," Misty offered.

He caught her gaze and she sent him a dazzling little smile. A smile that said she might have been refraining from offering a similar answer. Oh what he would have given to see the waiter's expression if she had said it, delivered in that perfect, oh-so-proper little accent of hers.

He really had to get them out of here.

"Nothing for me, either," he said, and handed the waiter a couple of twenties. "Keep the change."

"Now see here—" Misty began.

"Thanks," the waiter said, smart enough to beat it with his generous tip before Misty could get another word in.

Tucker stood and extended his hand.

She folded hers in her lap. "I am more than capable

of paying for a meal, or a taxi for that matter. I must insist that we discuss this entire arrangement.''

He simply reached down and took her hands from her lap and pulled her to her feet. ''No rules, you said.''

''I believe I added the caveat that we'd only do something if we both agreed.''

''I thought you just meant when we were naked.'' He didn't bother to keep his voice down.

She sent him a look that would have withered a duke, or whatever. ''Oh, honestly.'' She snatched her hand from his and pushed past him.

He was right behind her, leaning close and whispering, ''I love it when you get in a snit. It makes me hot.''

She whirled around and glared in the face of his wide grin. ''I do not get into snits.''

He merely raised his eyebrows.

Her lips twitched then. ''You're insufferable, you know.''

''So I've been told.''

''So I would imagine.''

He couldn't help it. He simply had to taste her. Right there on the sidewalk, diners looking on. He pulled her close before she knew what he was about. Whatever she'd been about to say was muffled by his mouth coming down on hers.

She started to pull away, but he was lost at the first taste of her. His hands gentled. His mouth did not. Then she sighed and relaxed into the kiss, her arms drifting to his shoulders, and he forgot the rest of the world existed.

She might claim to have a few things to learn, but kissing wasn't one of them. He quickly discovered she knew her way around a man's mouth. God have mercy. He finally forced himself to break away. It was that or give new meaning to the term "dining al fresco."

He took one last little taste of her bottom lip— "dessert," he murmured—then let her go. "Next meal we have is your treat, okay? And you can pay for the cab anytime you want."

"Um—" Her eyes were a bit unfocused, her lips all soft and thoroughly kissed. She cleared her throat, moved farther away from the railing circling the café tables. "Fine, that will be fine."

Tucker ducked inside and asked the first waiter he saw to call another taxi, then met her at the curb. He cupped her elbow, leaned in close. "Do we need to discuss public displays of seduction?"

"No," she said, her bearings somewhat restored. "I believe we've covered that quite well already."

He grinned and turned her so she faced him. "So, any voyeuristic fantasies on your list?"

She gave him a saucy little smile. "As it happens, that little scene back there notwithstanding, no. You?"

"No. But that accent of yours is making me rethink my feelings on dominatrix scenarios."

Now that was quite a wicked gleam. It made those gemstone eyes all but shoot sparks. He enjoyed the hot slice of pleasure that snaked down his spine. He'd always been more of an equal opportunity guy in bed, but the more he was around her, the more he felt his boundaries expanding.

"You were right, about me not wanting to order my subjects about, as it were," she said, those sparks so deliciously at odds with the haughty tone, "but I'll certainly take your interest under advisement."

The cab pulled up then and he helped her in. Her hands were so pale and perfect, her fingers slender, her nails short but a tender pink. He knew that, despite her English rose appearance, there was nothing remotely fragile about her, and yet he felt this incredible need to be gentle. Like she was something exquisitely delicate that he'd never risk marring in any way. He climbed in beside her, imagining his harder, bigger body, covering her smaller, more refined one.

This led to images of her astride him, all that translucent skin sinking down over his darker, thicker—

"Where to?" the cabbie asked.

Misty glanced at him questioningly.

"The Bellagio." If the tightness in his voice gave away his thoughts, oh well. God, everything he had was tight. And what wasn't tight was almost painfully hard.

This time she took his hand, slipped her fingers through his and gave him a light squeeze. It was almost as if she was reassuring him, which should have been ludicrous. Except her touch *was* reassuring. They were well and truly in this together.

They rode in silence. Her gaze averted out the window, giving him ample time to study her, to think about what they were about to do. It struck him that whereas he'd normally just go with the flow, make sure everyone involved had a good time before going on their merry way...he was already worried about how long she was going to stay, what he'd do if she decided to leave after this afternoon. Which was ridiculous considering he hardly even knew her. Had barely tasted her.

If ever a chance to have a wild no-strings affair were to present itself, this was certainly it. And it had been her idea! So the last thing he should be concerned with was where it would lead.

To the airport, he thought. *With separate flights taking us our separate ways.*

He looked down at their joined hands and tried to remember all the reasons why never seeing her again would be a good thing. Even one would help.

The cab slowed and pulled into the wide entrance to the hotel. The stunning fountain display sent water thrusting skyward in rocketing, crystalline pillars, all in an artistic pattern meant to awe. He didn't even notice. He was more involved watching her, wondering where her thoughts were.

She turned to him just then, as the cab slowed to a stop. That saucy grin had resurfaced. "You know, I never thought of fountains as being particularly phallic, however all that spouting and surging has rather carnal overtones, don't you agree?"

Tucker had to laugh at himself. Here he was pondering fates and futures...and she was focused on their real reason for being together. Their only reason.

Her lips quirked. "Why the dubious look? Having sudden performance anxiety?" She paid the cabbie and slid out of the car after him, then glanced pointedly at the arc of fountains thundering skyward. "Don't worry, I don't have any grand illusions."

Tucker decided he could worry about what might have been later. Right now he wanted to join her in the fun. To that end, he snagged her arm as she whirled away from him and spun her neatly around...and full up against him. "Maybe you should."

Her eyes went round as her hips collided with his. "My, my," she managed. "Perhaps I should indeed."

He escorted her inside, completely unaware of the grandiose lobby, the glass flowers overhead. He only had eyes for her. Somehow they managed to find their way to the bank of elevators. He pushed the up button, but she was tugging his hand away.

"Wait a minute."

"Having second thoughts?"

She shook her head, her lips curving in a smile that could only be deemed naughty. "No, just thinking there was something on that list you spoke of, something I've always wanted to do."

His own lips curved. "In the elevator? Well, as a matter of fact, that's something I—"

"No," she said, "though we must discuss that further." She tugged his arm and ducked around the corner, nodding to the door marked Stairs.

"Ah." He pulled the heavy door open and they both slipped inside. All the noise and hubbub of the lobby evaporated the instant the door clicked shut. Tucker glanced up the utilitarian stairwell. "What floor did you say you were on?"

"Top floor. Penthouse suite."

That raised an eyebrow. "You do sell a lot of books."

"I do," she said matter-of-factly, "but I owe this particular decadence to Lucas Blackstone. I don't know how he found out I didn't go to the airport, probably the driver. But there were explicit instructions to upgrade my accommodations."

"Hell of an upgrade."

She shrugged and laughed. "What can I say?"

"And you give me grief for wanting to buy you lunch."

She stepped in closer, toyed with the top button of his shirt. "I'm not planning to seduce Lucas Blackstone. And, for the record, I did decline his hospitality. The staff of the hotel insisted, and I do so try to avoid making a scene."

Tucker liked the feeling of her fingers brushing against his throat. In fact, he liked her brushing against any part of him. "How very thoughtful of you, then."

"Yes, how very," she responded, somewhat distractedly. Her focus was on his shirt, specifically the way it fit his chest and shoulders, which she was presently testing by smoothing her palms over them.

"Exactly—" He had to pause, clear his throat. "Exactly what is your stairwell fantasy?"

She smiled up at him. "Oh, nothing in particular. I just want to experience that dangerous thrill of possibly being caught." She slipped around him and danced up the first couple of stairs.

He remained at the base. "No voyeuristic tendencies, huh?"

"Oh no, I don't want anyone to actually watch, or even catch us. It's just knowing they could."

He rested his hand on the railing, propped his foot on the bottom step. "Which means they might. Then what?"

She danced up a few more steps, stopping on the landing. "Well, if they couldn't there wouldn't be the thrill of discovery, would there? The risk is the point."

He moved up one step. "And I'm asking what happens if you get caught? Headlines, bad press…"

She laughed. "Authors enjoy the anonymity of having well-known names, but largely unrecognizable faces. So, if we get caught, well…" She shrugged. "I'll make something up. It *is* what I do."

Tucker underscored the mental note to find a book-store later. He wanted to learn all there was to know about her. Certainly something of who she was showed in her work. It couldn't be entirely fictional if it came from her mind. If nothing else, it would help him understand some of her fantasies. Of course, a few hours from now, he might not need her books to learn that.

"How very wicked," she mused as he smiled. "What naughty little thought just crossed your mind?"

He charged the stairs, making her yelp and run up the next flight. "Hey," he said, hitting the landing and starting up the next step. "Is chasing you part of this? Because I need to know just how many floors it's supposed to take. I have to pace myself if you want me to actually be able to do anything when I finally catch you.''

She leaned over the railing, one floor up. ''You run up stairs for a living, don't you, Fire Marshal Greywolf? And this time you've got no gear. And the building's not even on fire.'' Now she was the one with the wicked grin. ''Just me.''

''Oh, okay. So that's how you want to play.'' He took to the stairs, grinning. She was right about his level of fitness. Although he didn't fight fires anymore, just investigated them after the fact, he still maintained the standards of any firefighter. You never knew when you'd be put to the test.

Of course, he thought, as he took the next flight two at a time, at this pace he wouldn't want to test his sexual prowess after thirty-plus flights. Still…she definitely knew how to get his adrenaline going. After another two flights, he slowed. Not because he needed to conserve energy, but because he was discovering the chase to be a bit of a turn-on himself and he didn't want to end it too soon.

Her breathless laughter floated down to him, spurring him on. Three flights later, he cornered her on a landing, midfloor. ''Madam,'' he said, his tone one of playful warning, ''do you realize this area is off-limits?''

Her eyes sparkled as he advanced on her. ''I—I didn't realize, sir.''

He boxed her into the corner. ''Oh, but I think you do. Otherwise, why did you run when I came into the stairwell?''

Her pupils expanded. Her nipples jutted tightly

against the soft weave of her top. "I didn't know who you were…what you might want from me."

He crowded her, until her back came up against the wall. "And just what did you think I wanted?"

Her breath was shallow and fast. "I saw you. Earlier. Watching me."

"I can't take my eyes off of you," he said, quite honestly. "You captivate me."

"It—you looked so…"

"Hungry?" He braced his arms on the wall beside her head. "I was. Am."

"That's why I ran."

He stepped in closer, finding himself incredibly aroused when she trembled. He'd never role-played in his life, not sexually, and would have thought he'd feel silly. At the moment, there was nothing remotely silly about the raging hard-on he had. "You watched me, too." He lowered one hand to her face, traced her lips. "You licked these, like you wanted to lap something else."

She shuddered…and nodded.

"So why run? Did you think I'd hurt you? Force you to do something you didn't want to do?" He pushed the tip of his finger into her mouth. "How could I, when you so obviously want the same things I do?"

Her gaze was riveted on his…and then he felt the tentative swipe of her tongue along his finger. Her mouth worked, pulled him in deeper.

Now he was the one trembling. "Be careful," he warned her, not entirely sure he was role-playing any longer. "I've wanted you for a long time. You're playing with fire here. And I know all about fire. How easily it can rage out of control.''

A soft moan sounded in her throat and he was undone. He slid the finger from her wet lips and crushed his mouth to hers instead. Not waiting for an invitation, he pushed his tongue into her sweet, hot mouth, wanting to feel that softness contract around his tongue the way it had around his finger. Wanting even more to feel her softness contract around him. All of him.

Her hands skated up his chest. He took them and pinned them to the wall. Not because he needed to dominate, but because he didn't trust himself where her hands were concerned. Her touch did wild things to him. And right now, he was handling all the wild he could manage.

She stiffened for a brief moment when her wrists touched the wall, but his insistent kisses had her going limp again. When he finally lifted his mouth from hers, she whimpered. And damn if he didn't almost come in his pants. Jesus, he'd never seen a woman look so aroused, so wanton, so needy. And he'd never been so brutally aware that the man who'd gotten her that way was him. Role-playing or not, he didn't care.

''Don't move your hands,'' he commanded, having no idea what was driving him now beyond his need to taste more of her. He released her wrists, enormously pleased when she left them as he'd instructed. Dear God he was discovering some things about himself he'd never been aware of…but was too damned intent on having what he wanted to care much at the moment. He drew his hands slowly down her arms, over her shoulders, to her breasts.

She shuddered hard as he rubbed his fingertips over her protruding nipples. It wasn't enough. He had to taste them, to feel them between his lips. He plucked open the tiny row of glass beads holding her top together. How quaint and reserved they were. But what he discovered when he parted the soft folds of her top was anything but.

"Good God have mercy," he breathed. She wore a demicup bra, with her nipples all but spilling out over the low-cut front. Had she been sitting there next to him at the police lab, across from him at lunch, all demure and proper...with this little piece of sin on underneath? Of course, she hadn't intended on going to the lab...she'd worn this to come and see him.

Well, he was seeing it now. Lord, was he seeing.

"Sir," she whispered, her voice tight, scratchy. "Please, just the feeling of your breath—"

Sir. He'd forgotten all about their little game. Would have thought her reminder would have been irritating, unnecessary. It had the exact opposite effect. It only served to jack him up higher, liberated him, in a sense, from analyzing this animalistic response she elicited in him. But there was something even more carnal in combining reality with the fantasy. "You wore this for me."

She said nothing.

So he blew a warm breath across her nipples, making her gasp. "Didn't you."

She nodded.

"Say it."

"Yes. Yes, I did."

"You wanted me to see your nipples grow hard, wanted me to be aware of the effect I have on you." He dipped his head, drew the very end of his tongue across the engorged tip. She moaned, twitched, but remained still. "Didn't you?"

"Yes," she gasped.

"So soft," he said, "so sweet. You want me to taste them, don't you? You know how badly I want to taste them, don't you?"

"Yes. Yes." The note of pleading should have shamed him. It didn't. They were both being equally undone by this little scenario that was unfolding between them, and he was well aware she had to know this, too. Just as she knew she could end it at any time. But wasn't.

He dipped his head again, drew his tongue more slowly across first one nipple, then the next. He wasn't even certain who groaned. "Incredibly sweet."

"More," she begged.

"Yes," he agreed, "I want more. You have no idea the hunger you've aroused in me." He slipped his lips over one pebbled nub, pulled it into his mouth and suckled as she shuddered with pleasure, then helped himself to the other, until her whimpering and moans had his own knees going decidedly weak.

His fingers twitched with the need to pull her shirt and bra entirely off, get past the bewitching way those soft cups lifted and offered her to him. The rest of him twitched with the need to yank her skirt up and find out if the rest of her was as soft and delicious as her pale white breasts. But in some fogged corner of his mind, her fantasy, her reason for starting this, crept back to the forefront.

It took considerable willpower, but he edged away from her, took her hands from the wall, and pulled them down in front of her, which served to push her sweet breasts even higher, almost managing to spill them out all together.

He released her. "Walk up the stairs."

She looked honestly confused, her hands lifting to her shirt.

He shook his head. "Leave your shirt alone. You look beautiful, your breasts are so beautiful, it's a crime to cover them." He nodded. "Walk. In front of me."

He could see the shiver cross her skin, the thin throb of the vein in her temple. The pulse beat at the base of her throat, which was perfectly pale. She wasn't nervous then, just as incredibly turned on as he was. It only enhanced the rush he felt, knowing he had her trust.

She held his gaze a moment longer, then just when he thought she might call a halt to this game after all, she turned and began to climb.

He stepped right in behind her. "Do you know how hard I am for you?"

She said nothing, just kept climbing.

He reached up, traced his fingers lightly down the crease of her buttocks through the seam of her long, slim skirt. She twitched, paused, continued.

"Are you wet for me?"

She said nothing, but paused at the next landing

when he gripped her hips from behind. He stepped up onto the landing behind her, walked her forward until she was pressed up against the wall, until she gasped when the cool glossy paint on the cement met her bared skin.

"I said," he murmured into her ear. "Are you wet for me?" He purposely didn't press his erection against her, though God knew it took admirable restraint not to.

"Yes," she said, quite calmly. "Very wet."

"I could take you right here, right now."

"Yes," she said, somewhat less calmly. "You could."

"I could push up that skirt of yours, slide right into you, and you'd welcome me. All of me."

"Yes," she said. This time it was almost guttural.

"Your screams, when I make you come, would echo. Anyone floors above, or floors below, would hear you climax."

He felt her breaths began to shorten, her lean body tense. He couldn't help it, he instinctively shifted his hips forward, pressed every raging inch against her. He barely swallowed his groan.

He slipped his hands around her waist, slid them up, pulled her back against him, so he could roll her nipples between his fingers, even as their hips were pressed tight against the landing wall. "Is that what you want?" he breathed in her ear. It wasn't what he thought he'd have wanted, taking her in a bare, cold stairwell, when there was a soft bed waiting for them a mere elevator ride away. And yet what was driving him now was not comfort, not even civility. If she said yes, he'd be out of his pants and buried deep before he could take another breath.

Just then the squeal of a metal door swinging open just above them ripped through air that moments ago had all but pulsed with sex.

Neither of them jumped, they both froze. Only the sounds of their heavy breaths disturbed the air, now rapidly cooling. Two men, talking. And they were coming down.

Tucker spun Misty around, immediately began to fumble with her buttons, but he was hopelessly thick fingered, too worried about her imminent embarrassment to be nimble. As the men hit the stairs leading down to their landing, she took matters into her own hands, quite literally, and drew Tucker into her arms and kissed him.

He distantly heard the chatter between the two men break off, then an uncomfortable silence as they hurriedly jogged down the stairs past the amorous couple.

Just as Tucker lifted his head, they both heard the light chuckle as the two men let themselves out at the next floor down.

Tucker locked gazes with Misty, then they both burst out laughing.

"Well," she said, smoothing her hair and rebuttoning her shirt, albeit with a slightly shaky hand. "I'd say we're off to a smashing start." She glanced up at him. "Wouldn't you?"

Tucker was still trying to collect himself, assimilate just how rapidly the two of them had let things get out of control. Way out of control. Dear God, had he really been about to take her right here in the stairwell? What if he had, and those two men had come through that door five minutes later?

Misty's eyes were dancing, her grin downright devilish. "But we didn't, and they didn't," she said, obviously reading his thoughts. She leaned in, her voice taking on a more Cockney slant. "What's a little stairwell seduction without the risk, eh, govnuh?"

Tucker had to laugh. "I'm not sure who's getting the lessons here."

She looped her arm through his and they started up the stairs together. "You said you wanted to explore, too. It's more fun when we're both entering uncharted ground together, don't you agree?"

"Yeah," he said, unsure he agreed with anything of the sort. They popped out the door at the next landing and he steered her directly to the elevators. "It's a real rush." Which was exactly what terrified him. Because it had been. And he thought he might easily become addicted. To the rush. And to her.

8

MISTY STEPPED into the elevator, clinging to the insouciant bravado that had gotten her through the inglorious finale of their little stairwell scenario. If she thought too much about where they might have been when those men had come through that door a few minutes later... She leaned forward and pressed the button for the penthouse, hiding the naughty smile that caught at the edges of her mouth.

Okay, so maybe it wasn't all bravado. And maybe it had been every bit as outrageously titillating as she'd fantasized something like that might be. And maybe, just maybe, she wasn't all that embarrassed, much less mortified, by their close call. A fact that she attributed more to the man she'd been with, than to any real moxie of her own.

He'd made her feel...safe. Taken care of. And that had little to do with his mastery of his role...and of her. With him the adventure hadn't been ridiculous. It had been highly erotic. She rubbed at her arms, thinking of what might lie ahead.

"Cold?"

She shook her head. The last word she'd use to describe any part of her at the moment was cold. "I'm fine." *Fabulous, amazed, in awe of what we almost just did.* A quick glance told her he was thinking similar thoughts. He had quite the wicked twinkle in his eye.

There were three other people in the car with them, but even with the primal thrill of what they'd just been doing to one another still coursing through her blood, she didn't dare push him—or herself—to test any other boundaries. Not public ones anyway. She'd pushed that envelope quite far enough for one day. Not that it diminished the tension in any way. He stood so near, she swore she could feel the heat pumping off of him. Or maybe it was just her.

To have him that close, know what it felt like to have his hands on her, his mouth on her…and not be touching him now…. She surreptitiously rubbed her thighs together to assuage the throb that pulsed there. It only managed to make it worse.

Just then she felt his fingers brush against her thigh. They crept up, slowly, until they teased the tips of her fingers. She glanced at him, but he was looking straight ahead, expression fixed in the standard elevator stare. They might as well have been complete strangers.

Except for what he was doing to her hand, slow strokes up and down her fingers, a light brush across her palm with his thumb. He toyed with her, almost, but not quite weaving his fingers between hers, almost but not quite pressing his palm to hers, light little brushes along her thigh all the while. Misty had never really thought about how erogenous hands could be…at least not on the receiving end. If she hadn't been so caught up wondering how those hands would feel doing similar things to the rest of her body, she might have made some mental notes for future scenes in her book.

But creating fiction was the last thing on her mind at the moment. Doing. That's what was on her mind. Experiencing. Submersing. Hell, wallowing. The elevator car paused several floors below the top and all three people got off. As the doors slid shut, Misty felt a spurt of anticipation at what he would do to her now that they were alone. But as the car climbed upward, he did nothing, other than what he had been doing for the past twenty floors.

It occurred to her then, like some great epiphany, that maybe he was waiting for her to do something.

I try something, then you try something. Isn't that how we figure out what we want?

Well, hadn't *she* been the one to drag him into that stairwell? Of course, she had to admit he'd taken it from there. And quite amazingly well, as it so happened. But then the car pulsed to a stop and the doors slid silently open.

"Well," she breathed. "We've arrived."

"So we have."

Suddenly flustered and feeling a bit ridiculous about it, she stepped out of the car and away from him, digging in her purse for her room card. She supposed she should be happy to even still have her purse. It could have slid off her shoulder at any time back in that stairwell and she doubted she'd have noticed.

She finally spotted the card and pulled it out with a sound somewhat like that of a person who'd just hit the jackpot. Catching his amused smile, she had to smile herself. "I know, it's silly to be so disconcerted…considering. Isn't it?"

She stepped over to her door and slid the room key in the slot. Tucker's hand came around from behind her to cover hers as she pulled the card free.

"You know, we can just order up a meal, or look at the view," he said. His breath was warm along her neck, his body so close, so willing. She already knew what it felt like beneath her hands. Strong, hard, a supple flex of muscles. And he was all hers. All she had to do was—

"We—we just ate," she said, knowing she was stalling, knowing he'd let her. "Although it feels like it was hours ago we were at that café."

"Time doesn't seem to measure itself by normal standards when I'm with you."

She turned a bit, took his hand and turned it over, folded her fingers between his. "The reason I wanted to come straight here earlier, was because of that."

He tugged the handle of her door, pushed it open, backwalked her into the marble foyer, not even glancing beyond her to the elegant Italian design. As always, his attentions were focused exclusively on her. She wondered if he had any idea what an aphrodisiac that was, then figured he must. For him this was merely an exciting interlude, and he was certainly going to do everything he could to maximize its potential. After all, she was doing the same thing.

Except…

"I didn't want to go to lunch first, because I didn't

want to get to know you better," she blurted as he moved her smoothly up against the foyer wall.

He paused, his hand halfway to her face. She almost whimpered when he lowered it again. *Fool*, she castigated herself. Why couldn't she just go with the flow, why did she always feel compelled to open her mouth and let spill forth whatever was in her mind? This wasn't the sort of lapse in decorum she'd wanted to indulge in.

"And you didn't think bringing me here, being intimate with me, was going to do that anyway?" He may have let his hand drop to his side, but he didn't move out of her personal space. He spoke calmly, that ever-present amusement still threading through his words, but there was an intensity vibrating between them as well.

Don't blow this, Misty. He's your best chance ever, so don't go ruining it. "There's a difference between sex, even hot sex, and intimacy."

"Ah," he said, the smile fully surfacing. The intensity didn't diminish however. If anything, it grew. "The upper crust accent returns."

She didn't know what to say to that. He was entirely too sensitive to her quirks for only having been around her so briefly.

"So, you wanted anonymous hot sex, then," he said. "You want me to be your fantasy lover, do all the things you feel are forbidden to you with your regular lovers-who-have-names-and-backgrounds."

"I know your name, your—"

"Rank and serial number." When she looked confused, he said, "The bare essentials. At most, that's all you know about me. That," he moved closer, but didn't touch her body with his, "and that I can make you want me."

"Yes," she said, her voice tight with that very want, "you can." She tried not to tremble when he finally lifted his hand, only to toy with the ends of her hair. She wanted more. Much, much more. "Is it so bad, being a fantasy lover? I know I might not fill your bill in that respect—" She broke off when he laughed in her face.

He braced his hands on either side of her head, grinning. "I don't know that I *have* a fantasy lover…never really wasted time with that." He moved closer, until he was pressing lightly against her, slid his hands down the wall until his arms were braced beside her head, his own mouth hovering dangerously close to hers. "But I can tell you that you've already done things to me that no one else ever has. In fact," he breathed, dipping in to kiss the corner of her mouth, "I'll lay awake at night for sure, replaying every second of what we just did in that stairwell."

He kissed the other corner of her mouth and dammit, she whimpered when he lifted his head without taking more.

"So then?" she managed. "Why don't we live the fantasy, as they say."

His mouth curved again, only there was something harder there this time, less gentle than she'd seen in him before. "Leave the real world out of it, you mean? Okay, sure. Why not? Pretend I'm whatever you want me to be. Butcher, baker…Indian chief."

He dipped his head again and she read his intent clearly this time.

She stopped him with a hand to his chest. "Wait. I didn't mean to insult—"

"No insult taken. But enough chitchat, right? Let's get down to it." He took her chin with definite intent, and angled his mouth over hers. There was no dancing this time, no teasing. He simply took.

And damn if he didn't make her want to take him right back. His tongue forged into her mouth like a hot brand, and there was nothing experimental in the way he went about seducing hers into doing the same. He didn't grind his hips into hers as she'd expected. Nothing so obvious as that, and yet the mere fact that he wasn't touching her except where their mouths mated was far more insidious to her self-control. Her hips pushed forward, seeking, her thighs felt molten, barely able to sustain her weight. The deeper he took the kiss, the more she wanted to claw his clothes from his body, pull him to the floor. Or just wrap her legs around his waist and—

No, no. It was exciting like this, no doubt about it. But even though he wasn't exactly angry, neither was he the man who'd charmed, seduced and teased her. It was one thing when they were role-playing, but this—this wasn't what she wanted. Jesus, just what in the bloody hell did she want?

She broke the kiss, managed to slip out from between him and the wall and stagger into the living room. He merely leaned in and pressed his forehead against the wall. They were both breathing heavily.

She absently let her purse slide off her shoulder

onto the nearest chair, and tried like hell to pull her wits about her. "I'm sorry."

"Do you want me to go?" he asked roughly.

She jerked her gaze back to him, but he was still leaning against the wall, head tucked, eyes averted. "No." It was the one thing she did know.

She tried like hell to make the words come together in her head the way she needed them to, and felt betrayed when they didn't. After all, she made her living with words, she felt she had a pact with them, that they'd be there for her always, as they always had been.

"Before..." she began falteringly, "when I said that thing about not wanting lunch. It was—" She dragged her hand through her hair, then dragged her gaze away from him. He was all tense, coiled like an animal reining in the urge to leap and strike. And she still harbored a few ideas about what it would be like if he did. To hell with charm.

"I suppose it goes to what you said, about time being an elastic quality where we're concerned," she said. "I don't know you, and yet I feel I know you, or at least feel connected to you, in some way that defies logic. If I spent more time with you, that... connection...would only strengthen. And this... this liaison between us, well, it isn't supposed to be about anything more than, than sex." *Dear Lord, you'd think she'd never been capable of stringing together a decent sentence in her life.*

He shifted, drawing her attention. Leaning one shoulder against the wall, he folded his arms across his chest. His expression was downright inscrutable, but that coiled tension remained. "I believe I was willing to forego the getting-to-know-you foreplay, as requested."

"Yes, yes you were." And quite handily almost did, she added silently. "But, well, there's a reason I've never done anything like this before. To those men-with-names-and-backgrounds," she added, her lips curving just a little. His did not. "It would have felt forced, put on. It didn't with you. And I suppose I didn't realize why until just now."

"Why?" He didn't move so much as a muscle, and yet she suddenly felt crowded.

"Role-playing is fine, to a point. But what you and I were just…" She shook her head, wishing she'd simply let him have her way with her. There was no way to explain without making herself vulnerable, which was exactly what she'd been trying to avoid. "Well, while I don't want to risk—"

"Developing more than lust for what I can do with you?" He pushed away from the wall. "To you?"

She couldn't rein in the tiny shudder that tightened the muscles between her legs. She drew herself up, determined to face him, to see this through, before they went a step further. "Yes, that's exactly it. But the fact is, I already do know you, at least a little…and it's precisely what I do know of you that makes it possible for me to do this in the first place." She backed up a step as he came closer. "So…so it's too late to be anonymous. And I don't want to pretend, not all the time. I—I want—"

He caught up to her then and her breath left her. She had no idea what she expected he'd do. Toss her over his shoulder? Ravish her where she stood? The look in his eye was so at odds with the always-smiling, devilish-gleam-in-the-eye man she'd lusted for since he first strolled into that room at Blackstone's. And yet, he wasn't playacting now either... and she discovered she was just as turned on by this side of Tucker Greywolf as any other.

So when he stopped just in front of her, and gently traced a finger along her lips, she almost fell apart completely. How could a man look so hard, be both hot and cold... and so exquisitely gentle, all at the same time?

"I don't think you can be intimate without risk," he told her quietly. "And I'm talking emotional risk here. It sort of goes with the territory. At least it does for me."

The question was right there, and too compelling not to spill out. "Do you fall in love so easily then?"

"No. But I always believe it's possible." His fingers drifted to her chin, then along her neck and collarbone.

"Every time?"

His gaze came up to hers. "Absolutely. Especially when I least suspect it."

"Have you ever been?"

"No. Not really. Not the way I want to be. You?"

She shook her head, having no idea how she was managing to have this conversation at all when his touch was literally setting off a maelstrom of reaction inside her.

"You write about love," he said, "surely you believe in it?"

"I believe it exists, yes."

He tipped her chin up, searched her face. "But not for you?"

She managed a light shrug.

Then the smile surfaced again, only this time the light in his eyes was downright...well, predatory was the only word she could think of. "We're not going to be anonymous lovers, Misty. You're right, it's already too late for that."

She said nothing, didn't have to.

"Why don't we enjoy each other, ask the questions that come up, that beg to be answered. What's the worst that could happen?"

You could break my heart. The one piece of herself she'd managed to retain intact.

"Does it scare you so much?" he asked, when she remained silent.

"I don't want to get hurt. I don't want to hurt you."

"No one wants to be hurt. But playing it safe is what finally forced you to seek out Blackstone's, isn't it? Maybe it's time to take some risks, be daring."

She did find her smile then. "I believe I've been quite daring up to this point." Her smile faltered. "But I wasn't intending to gamble anything so precious as my heart."

He drew her closer, tipped her head back. "Then we'll just have to take very good care of one another, won't we?" He leaned down, until his mouth was a whisper away from hers. "But there's only so much safeguarding we can do, you know. So tell me to leave now, Misty. It's the only way to be certain you'll stay safe.''

And that's when she knew it was already too late. She'd long since crossed that line and hadn't even been aware of doing it. She reached for him then, framed his face and tilted his mouth so it would fit hers the way she knew it fit best. ''Don't leave,'' she told him, praying she wouldn't be begging him for the same thing four days from now.

9

As she pulled him into a deep kiss of her own initiation, Tucker told himself he'd have turned and walked out the door without looking back if she'd asked him to.

Thank God she hadn't put him to the test.

Damn but Amethyst Fortuna Smythe-Davies knew how to kiss a man.

She teased her tongue into his mouth and he groaned. Sweet, so damn hot and sweet. He pulled her close, taking her hips in his hands, pushing what was so hard against all of her incredible softness. Now it was her moaning, and him twitching and throbbing. Need, had he ever felt such an intense need? This went well beyond the foreplay they'd indulged in on those stairs.

He hadn't paid any attention to the design of her suite, beyond that she was in it. He had no idea where the bed was, but he felt the thickly cushioned arm of a loveseat pressing against the back of his thighs. He rocked back, taking her with him as he slid over the side, landing on his back.

Her eyes widened in surprise, but were already drifting shut again as she came down on top of him and he pulled her head to his. He never wanted to stop tasting her, was determined to have his mouth on some part of her for as long as she'd allow…or as he could make her want to allow. He seduced her tongue back into his mouth, suckled her until her hips began to move on his.

He slid his hands down the side of her thighs, then back up, taking her skirt with him. "So smooth," he murmured, "so strong." She straddled him, bent low so their mouths and tongues could continue their dance. Her breasts brushed along his chest and he found he desperately wanted to feel those taut nipples skim over his bare skin. He reached for the hem of her shirt, only to find her hands there, holding him back.

Thwarted, but easily diverted, he buried his hands in her hair, took the kiss deeper, until they were both panting. She pressed harder against him, riding him, and he tried again to pull at her shirt. "I want to see you, feel you on me."

She shook her head, pushed his hands away, this time capturing his wrists and pulling them over his head. "Not yet," she finally managed, ending on a little gasp as he bucked his hips.

She gave him a "no funny business" look, which was hilarious considering the funny business they were hip deep in, but he reined in his control and made every effort to still himself beneath her. Her expression shifted to a considering smile, which made him wonder what creative little thoughts were going on behind those gemstone sparklers of hers.

He honestly couldn't help the little hip buck that followed. After all, he was only human.

She tightened her hold on his wrists, blowing a stray brown curl from her damp cheek. "Wait."

"You keep grinding on me like that, and there might not be a later to wait for."

She grinned. "Now, now. It's my turn to do a bit of the torturing."

Like this wasn't, he wanted to ask. Instead he raised an eyebrow. "Torture?" He clenched his jaw against the growl that threatened when she squeezed his hips between her thighs and pushed down with a little rotation of her hips. "We're not talking pain here, are we?"

She released him and sat up, a satisfied smile on her face when he left his arms draped over his head. "Are you in pain, now?"

"Define pain."

She laughed. "I assume you meant pain of the more sadistic sort."

"There are some who'd say this almost qualifies. But yes, that's what I meant. You didn't have any S&M fantasies lurking about on that list of yours, did you?"

"No whips and studded leather if that's what you mean. I'm a bit of a wimp when it comes to that sort of thing." She eyed him. "Disappointed?" She wiggled a little as she settled atop him.

He could only shake his head.

"Good." She stayed upright and toyed with the hem of her shirt. "There is one thing I've wanted to try, however. Which is why I stopped you."

"If it's how to make a man harder than he thought possible," he gritted out, "you've aced that course."

She laughed, provoking a long, low growl from him as her thighs tightened further. "No, no. Stripping."

"Stripping," he repeated, fighting hard to keep his hands off her. She kept toying with the hem of her top, giving him tiny peeks of pale, creamy midriff. He curled his fingers into fists above his head.

"Not the sort that takes place in sleazy nightclubs with music and a pole," she clarified.

"A real shame, that," he said, imitating her British lilt.

She merely grinned, the light flush making her milky skin positively glow. "I'll confess right now, I'm not much of a dancer."

He bucked his hips lightly, making her gasp. "Could have fooled me."

She leaned forward, bracing her palms on his chest. "No doing that, I'm not finished with you yet."

"Oh, you're closer to the finish line than you think."

She sat back up, no longer rotating those sweet hips of hers, but bringing him to the edge nonetheless. She fingered the hem of her shirt. "So I should just leave this on, then?"

"Absolutely not. As long as you stop that—" He made a whirling motion with his hand.

She wiggled on him. "This?"

"Yeah," he groaned, tipping his head back, centering every ounce of will he had on controlling himself. "That."

"Ah."

He peered at her from one open eye. "Think you're real cute, don't you?"

"I think I want to take my shirt off, is what I think."

He grinned through clenched teeth. Her royal highness was back. "And I'm not stopping you, but I do have one question."

"Which is?"

He opened both eyes. "You've never taken your clothes off for a man before?"

"Well, there's a difference between removing one's garments for the purpose of lovemaking...and stripping them off as a point of pleasure all on its own."

"Damn but I love it when you get regal on me."

She laughed. "Sorry."

"Never apologize to me." He'd said it a bit more fiercely than he'd intended, but he didn't care. "Just be yourself."

"You mean the pathetic self that has never disrobed for a man in a provocative manner?"

He ignored her self-directed jab. "Why haven't you? I can't believe you never had the opportunity."

She shrugged. "I suppose it's simply never seemed appropriate. More like stage direction or something."

"And now?"

She settled then, met his gaze. "And now it doesn't."

He couldn't recall ever feeling so gratified. "Thank you."

She gave him a saucy wink. "Don't thank me yet, you haven't seen the performance." Without waiting for a reply, she pulled in a breath and seemed to pick a spot somewhere past his head and focus on it as she lifted her shirt. She stopped before she'd bared more than an inch of her midriff. "Bollocks."

"You were doing fine." He shifted. "Trust me. Or is this part of the act?"

She shook her head, looking down at him. "I think I should have started with something that didn't have an endless row of tiny buttons, something I could open without fumbling, slide off my shoulders. It's hard to be seductive yanking all this over one's head."

"Oh, I'm betting you'll manage."

She continued staring at him, but it was clear her thoughts had shifted elsewhere, puzzling out a solution.

Tucker thought that this was probably the expression she had when she went off inside her mind, crafting this bit of a story, or that. He was a little in awe of how she did that, created a whole world, filled with people, out of nothing more than wisps of ideas and images in her mind.

Then she was slipping off of him and perching on the edge of the heavy glass coffee table that fronted the padded couch.

"Whoa, wait—" He'd half rolled to a sit, but she pushed him back down.

"I'm not going anywhere," she said.

"You're not where you were."

"I think I've hit on a solution."

"So far, I'm not thinking much of it."

She merely gave him a look. "Patience."

He lay back down on the loveseat, head bracketed

in his hands. This was the damnedest roll in the hay he'd ever had with a woman. Not that he wished himself anywhere else at the moment. "You know, not to spoil this or anything, but most guys would be quite happy if you just ripped that shirt off over your head without all the fuss and bother. We don't care if it musses your hair and makeup. We're simple creatures."

She smiled, then shifted her perch so that her back was to him. "I've always thought so."

"Very funny."

"You've a point, though. Mostly I've undressed in the dark," she went on. "Or just dispensed with clothing sort of methodically. And you're right, I never had a complaint."

"You're not going to get any complaints from me, either." He tried very hard not to imagine her undressing for other men. Neither of them were inexperienced, and just because she wanted to try some new things with him didn't make her a novice. He knew all that. And yet, there was definitely some part of him that wanted to be the one she learned these new things with. And that same part balked at the idea of her going on to share them with others. He tried to ignore that part.

"It's not a tease I'm after, really," she said. "More like adding to the foreplay." She glanced over her shoulder. "And this is not to say that ripping one's clothes off doesn't have its place."

"Hear, hear."

"But for now," she went on, once again turning away from him, "I'd like to try something else. You tell me what you think.'' One more quick glance. ''Any suggestions or improvements are requested and appreciated.''

He laughed. ''Yeah, right. Talk about a guaranteed way to kill the mood. I've discovered that most women don't actually want a critique, no matter what they say.''

''I'm not most women.''

Well. She had him there.

''I'm a writer, I'm used to critiques.''

''Fine. I'll do my best.''

''No pretty lies,'' she warned. ''I don't need them.''

No, she very likely didn't. ''No lies.'' And, no matter that the motive wasn't entirely clear, he promised himself right then that no matter where this led, he would be honest. With her. With himself.

She slipped the edges of her shirt between her fingers, breathed a quiet sigh. ''Okay then,'' she said, more to herself than to him. Slowly, very slowly, she drew the hem upward, revealing the narrow span of her lower back. As creamy smooth as the rest of her. She angled her torso, slid the fabric higher. The thin silk strip of her bra appeared.

It was pale blue, which only made her skin seem more translucent. There was a supple play of her muscles as she continued to draw the shirt over her head. Her hair was swept up inside of it, so he could see the full, unadorned line of her back. It was graceful, a sinuous curve that had him tightening the fists he'd made of his hands. He'd thought his need to touch her was strong before, but now…

"This torture stuff," he managed. "You do it really well."

She paused, but said nothing, then slipped the clingy knit off entirely, so that her hair spilled out in a springy wave of silken curls that brushed down along her shoulders. How badly he wanted to lean over, slip his fingers beneath those silky blue straps and tug them down, then spin her around and pull her down on top of him.

"Misty…" he began, already tightening his muscles as he prepared to roll to a sit.

She shifted then, just enough to look at him over her shoulder.

The unintentional seductiveness of the pose, her shoulders bare, the lean line of her body, like a dancer, coiled and supple. Her eyes had rounded just slightly in question, her hair was mussed and tousled around her face, her lips still puffy from his kisses. The look of her arrested any movement he might have made. "Jesus, you're stunning."

She stilled, then breathed softly. "Thank you." Then, still looking at him, she slowly fingered one bra strap over the curve of her shoulder, let it drop to carelessly brush her upper arm. He'd seen the front of that bra, the demicups, so incredibly sexy. He was amazed how one thin strip of silk dangling on her arm could make him even hotter.

Then she shifted on the table until she was kneeling on it, facing him, her slim skirt taut around her thighs as she sat back on her heels…creamy skin spilling out of that demibra, nipples hard and begging for his mouth.

Tucker fought twin urges to stroke her…and himself. The need to find some relief was overwhelming. But he kept his hands as they were, locked tightly above his head, braced there as surely as if she'd handcuffed him.

And that image proved dangerous, as it only made him think of doing the same to her, kneeling in front of him, wrists restrained, nipples freed for his tongue.

The image was wiped from his mind the instant she slipped the other strap off her shoulder. Her arms, crossed in front of her chest, kept her bra from spilling off and freeing her breasts to him completely.

''Take it off, Misty,'' he said, unaware of how commanding he sounded. All he heard was the need. He was almost desperate with it.

She merely smiled. He wanted to snarl. Foreplay be damned. Torture didn't begin to measure what she was doing to him. Payback was going to be hell. He'd make sure of it. Only he wasn't entirely sure she'd be all that upset about it. Neither would he, come to think of it.

Then she was slowly peeling the skim of pale blue lace downward, fully revealing those taut nipples, surrounded by bud pink areolas that had filled his mouth so perfectly. Dear God had he ever seen skin so perfect, so unkissed by the sun? Kissed only by him.

He'd always been drawn toward fiery, darker women. Believing the darker the skin, the hair, the eyes, the more passionate the temperament.

Now she had him reassessing all his beliefs.

She let the cups tip forward as she reached behind her back to unhook the bra.

Tucker was moving before he realized his intent. She leaned away, so he took her hips, turned her until her back was to him. "Let me." He brushed her hands away and gently undid the hooks, letting the wisp of silk and lace fall to the floor.

He dropped his hands, but remained seated on the edge of the couch, just behind her, almost, but not quite touching any part of her. "Anticipation," he said softly, his breath stirring a wisp of her hair. "Is hell." He lifted her hair and leaned in to kiss the base of her neck. She trembled. "And heaven."

He slid her hair to the side, continued his exploration around the base of her neck, drifted his lips along her collarbone, stopping to nip gently at her shoulder. "Exquisite."

Her breathing was shallow, unsteady. It took every bit of his own ragged control to keep from pulling her to the floor, to continue this slow assault, knowing they'd eventually get to where he so badly wanted to be. "You taste…" He couldn't find the word, so he simply continued to savor the softness that was her. He nudged her head back, so it rested on his shoulder, allowing him access to her earlobe, the edge of her jaw.

Her hands came up to cover herself, though to his surprise and increased arousal, not from shyness, but from need. She pressed her palms against the tight buds her nipples had become, shuddering lightly as he drew the tip of his tongue along the shell of her ear.

Watching her touching herself as he tasted her was almost too much. He circled his arms around her waist, slid his palms across her abdomen, then upward. She went to move her hands, but he covered them instead. ''Do what you need, take what you need,'' he murmured against her neck.

''I need you. Touching me.'' She slid her hands from beneath his, then pressed his palms against her breasts. Shuddering, she said, ''Yes,'' the word a vibrating growl.

Her body leaned heavily back into his, her head rolling on his shoulder as he rubbed his palms lightly back and forth across her nipples. When he rolled them between his fingers, she arched and cried out. He thought he might have too, he was so damn close.

He fastened his mouth on her neck, wanting to roll those hard nubs between his lips. She continued to writhe beneath the twin attentions of his hands and his mouth, until his control snapped. He slid back to the loveseat, pulled her with him until she lay sprawled on her back across his lap, her legs splayed across the table. ''I need to taste you. All of you.''

She looked up at him, eyes a deep violet. ''Please.''

He lowered his mouth to hers, took her deep into a hard, rough kiss. There was no finesse left in him, no patience. He tore his mouth from hers, breathing hard, but needing more than just her soft lips. He lowered his mouth to her breasts, to those sweet puckered nubs. He laved her, suckled her, took her into his mouth until she was arched and clawing the air. His need was a clawing thing as well.

He needed to feel all of her. She was already rolling to face him, aligning her body with his as they slid down into the cushions. It wasn't enough, the loveseat too short to accommodate them. He wanted more, needed more.

He kept her plastered to him and sat up, spun his feet to the floor even as he shoved her skirt up so she could straddle his lap. Finally, she was pressed against where he so badly needed to feel her. She all but ripped his shirt open. They both groaned as skin finally met heated skin. He pressed her close, and it still wasn't close enough. She was moving on him, he felt like something live, hot and molten, had been pumped into him. He was on fire. And he knew all about fire.

Pants, why in the hell was he still wearing pants, goddammit. But he couldn't put thought to deed. They were both grinding at each other, seeking what they were beyond needing. He'd taken her mouth again, she'd taken his with her tongue, branded him, beguiled him, consumed him.

He had his fingers buried in her hair, kissing her like he'd never kissed anyone. Her hands slid between them, tugged at the waistband of his pants. Somehow, with him pushing, her pulling, they managed to slide everything down his thighs.

His breath caught, held, as she freed him, the air brushed him…then, before he could question her, question himself, think a single clear thought, she was there, sliding down over him. Slow, they should be going slower, he thought wildly, it was going to be over before it began. But that wildfire in his blood had caught and had already rampaged out of control. He was already thrusting deep before he could form a single thought. She was so sweet, so damn wet, tight. And she moved on him like a dancer, coaxing his hips to match hers. And they did, effortlessly.

He took her mouth hungrily. It was as if he couldn't bury enough of him inside of her, he wanted more. And more. She was grunting—or maybe it was him—as they bucked harder and harder. Now her hands were in his hair, pulling as she bit his lower lip. Even the pain was somehow exquisite.

And then she was growling, pushing harder, squeezing tighter…and he shot, like fire fed with a sudden burst of oxygen, right through the roof. The shout as he climaxed was literally ripped from somewhere deep inside his soul.

He almost came off the cushions he bucked so hard, thrust so high. She grabbed at the back of the loveseat to stay with him, little panting squeals came from her as he pounded his way through the climax. Waves, it was like great shuddering waves.

"Jesus," he breathed, wondering if his heart was going to slow before it split right through his chest.

She slowed, relaxed her grip a little, but didn't stop moving on him. If he was capable of speech, he'd apologize for getting there first, tell her he wanted to keep going, but was pretty sure every body part he had was paralyzed.

Her head tipped back as she arched, instinctively seeking what she still needed. Somewhere he found the ability to move. He gripped her hips, slid her from him. She whimpered in protest. He wasn't all that happy to leave her either.

"Shh," he managed, his throat and tongue dry from all that panting and groaning. He'd never been particularly vocal during sex. A smile curved his lips. He imagined that was about to change. Again, they'd both found their something new.

He lifted her from his lap, leaned forward until he could nudge her onto the coffee table. She was climbing up from the fog they'd both descended into. He didn't want her to. Not yet.

His pants and briefs were around his ankles—for Christ's sake—which inhibited him further, but he managed. Sliding to the floor on his knees, he shifted her around. "Lay down."

"But…" He gently pushed and she gave in, her muscle control apparently as rubbery as his. She shivered as the glass met her heated skin and started to sit up. He pushed her down.

"Only part of you is going to cool off, trust me. Lay back."

Her eyes blinked open, her head lolled toward him as she struggled to focus. "Tucker…" The word was thick, hoarse.

"I'm here, let me…you're not done yet."

A lazy smile came over her face. "Oh, I'm fine. Later. For me. Later."

He shook his head. "Now." As he spoke, he brushed his palm across her stomach, then dipped his head and took one soft nipple into his mouth…as he dipped his fingers between her legs.

She tensed slowly, then arched exquisitely as he continued. Her gasps turned into low moans, and then back into gasps as she gathered up.

"Come for me, Misty. Take me. Take what you want." He slid his fingers into her, slowly, then back out, all the while flicking at her now tightened nipples with his tongue. "Yes," he growled against her damp skin as she tightened around his slick fingers, cried out and bucked hard against him, again, then again.

When her head finally rolled toward him, he shifted, slid from her, took her mouth. Her arms, boneless, slid around his neck, tugging him closer. "Mmm," was all she could manage.

Finally he eased back and she opened her eyes. They stared at each other for several long seconds. A slow smile curved her lips. "So."

"So." He grinned. "Pretty raving magnificent for a first go at it, eh?"

"You do a very bad British accent," she said lazily.

"I'll strive to improve."

"Might kill me." She closed her eyes, then smiled as she stretched and twitched just a little with one last tiny spasm. "But okay, if you insist."

And just like that, he wanted her again. Not that his body was close to cooperating, but if it could... "Shower?" At least then he could keep his hands on her.

"That would require moving."

"I could carry you."

She slid her gaze to his. "Could you now?"

"We firefighters are used to lugging lots of gear up many flights."

"Be still my girlish heart."

His grin widened a bit sheepishly. "I just compared you to heavy equipment, didn't I?"

Her eyes drifted shut. "One could interpret it that

way." She didn't sound too put out. "But if we're going to discuss heavy equipment..." She lifted one eyelid, glanced downward, then back up at him.

"No fair pumping my ego so smoothly when I was so—"

"Unsmooth? And I'd say we both pumped quite well."

He laughed and slid his arms beneath her and lifted her. "Ah, just right," he said.

She wrapped her arms around his neck. "Apology accepted."

He rolled back on his heels, tightening his hold on her as he stood up, only to pitch forward when the pants around his ankles hamstrung his movement. "Oh!"

But it was too late. As his knees smacked hard against the coffee table, Misty rolled from his arms, to the carpet beyond the coffee table, landing with a soft thud. And a giggle. "Apology rescinded."

10

"WELL, THAT WAS THE APEX of smoothness right there. Jesus, are you okay?" Tucker swore even as they both laughed. He leaned over the table as Misty sat up and pushed her hair from her face.

"That's what I get for doing this without a trained professional, I suppose." Her eyes were in full gemstone twinkle. "This would be where that warning 'don't try this at home' would likely come into play, don't you think?"

And it was right in that moment that Tucker thought he actually felt his heart tumble inside his chest. Was *this* what it felt like to fall in love?

His parents had been such a shining example of love and devotion, he'd always assumed the same would happen for him. But as the years mounted, he'd honestly begun to wonder if maybe they were the exception and he'd overromanticized the whole deal. At the moment, however, he wouldn't have been all that surprised to hear harps and violins. Maybe it was this simple after all. It just took meeting the right one.

"Actually," he said, for the moment putting off the potentially life-altering, not to mention dangerous sensation to postcoital hormone-induced infatuation, "the phrase that applies here is 'if at first you don't succeed, try, try again.'"

"Should I be so trusting then?"

"It's worked out pretty well so far, hasn't it?"

Her eyes darkened and a little sigh escaped. "There is that." A slow smile curved her lips. "However, perhaps you should pull your trousers up first," she admonished. "Or just take them off altogether."

"Top-notch idea," he said, grinning when she winced. "Okay, okay, I'll stop with the accent. Attempted accent," he added when she just gave him a look. "I can't help it. I love how the inflections reflect your mood. We should all have such a multidimensional tool at our disposal." He turned back to the loveseat and pried off his shoes, glancing back when he heard her snicker.

She waved a hand at him, trying not to laugh. "I'm sorry, it's too easy."

"What?" Then he replayed his words in his head and shook a finger at her. "Naughty, naughty girl."

She simply shrugged. "It's my job to think like that. Can I help it if I happen to excel in my chosen profession?"

"No. And with my heartfelt gratitude, I wouldn't have it any other way." He shifted his attention back to getting his shoes off, and found himself thinking that here he was, sitting half-naked, leaving cheek prints on a glass coffee table in a five-star penthouse suite…his pants down around his ankles, a mostly naked woman sprawled on the floor behind him—a woman he'd just met and made wild, uncontrollable love to…and he didn't feel the least bit awkward. About any of it. Quite the opposite in fact.

He slid his pants off and noticed his wallet had fallen out of his pocket at some point and bounced under the table. He reached for it at the same time she did.

"Here," she said, scooping it up first and handing it to him.

That's when it hit him. *Uncontrollable.* Dammit. "Thanks."

"What's wrong?"

"We—I didn't use any protection." He looked directly at her. "I'm sorry. I know it's a lame excuse now. I've never done that before. Ever." Hell, even as a hormone-crazed teenager he'd never done anything this stupid. "I'm healthy, if that helps. We get tested as part of department regulations."

Misty kneeled, wiggled her skirt down and moved to perch on the opposite side of the table, apparently as at ease with her partial nudity as he was. If he wasn't so busy beating himself up, he'd have found her level of comfort around him immensely gratifying.

"It's okay, Tucker. I mean, it's not all your responsibility. I take responsibility, too, here. I—"

"I *always* take care of things, always, but we— this—" He shook his head and would have sworn, but she was grinning and he couldn't help it, his lips twitched, too. "I've never been like this, the way I was with you. It was—"

"Incredible?"

"I was going to say insane, since I obviously was,

but yes, it was that, too.'' *And more.* The postcoital infatuation wasn't wearing off. If anything, that excuse was feeling flimsier by the second. ''Still, if there are any...complications, from this, from us, I want you to know, I—''

''I had a sponge in,'' she interrupted. Now she flushed a bit as she shrugged. ''When I left here earlier, I was heading to your place and...well, a girl can't be too careful. If it helps, I'm healthy, too. But there won't be any complications.''

He sighed in relief. For both of them. ''Still, I should have asked, should have—''

She covered his hand, then cupped his face in her palm. ''You really are a sweetheart, you know that,'' she said, looking into his eyes. ''Honorable and stalwart.''

He smiled and actually felt his skin begin to heat up. ''You're making me sound like a knight of the realm again. Trust me, my reputation back home is—''

''If you try to tell me you're some kind of cad—'' She broke off and laughed. ''Well, I suppose I should believe it, considering your proposition the night we met, not to mention what we were about just now and back in that stairwell.'' She rifled her fingers through his short hair. ''But I don't believe it. I suppose that's the fiction writer in me, eh?''

He closed his hand around hers and pulled it to his mouth, where he kissed her fingertips. It made her eyes widen, then soften. He'd remember that, and find ways to do that more often. She made him want to be stalwart and honest and all the things a woman like her would need to fall in love.

"Or perhaps it's because you professed such a strong belief in the possibility of love," she said, then swallowed hard and pulled away, as if she couldn't quite believe she'd said it.

Looking into her eyes just now, he actually had to bite back the urge to tell her his thoughts, that his belief in those very possibilities was growing by leaps and bounds. Could she be having the same revelations? Or was it, as she said, simply a flight of fancy she wanted to believe in? "It's only natural that a woman who writes about love would be a romantic. But trust me, I'm no hero, stalwart or otherwise. I'm just a regular guy."

"A regular guy who thinks nothing of running into burning buildings and sweeping women off their feet."

"A guy who used to run into burning buildings. Now the only buildings I go into are already done burning." He grinned. "And you can see how well I do on that sweeping thing."

"I believe I was off my feet."

They both laughed, but slowly quieted as their eyes met. He stroked her cheek. Suddenly it was important for her to know this wasn't a flight of fancy for him, but something more important. Or something that had the potential of being more important.

But she spoke first. "I, um, would you like to take that shower? Or a sauna?"

"We have options?" He grinned, happy enough for the moment that she wanted him to stay.

"Actually," she said conspiratorially, "there are two baths. A his and hers."

"Oh."

She laughed. "What, too lavish for you?"

"I'm just a simple country boy."

"Right. And I'm a sheltered English lass."

He pulled her across the table until she was draped over his lap. "Shall we use both his and hers? Or choose one and share?"

"I say we use both." She smiled. "One at a time."

"A practical English lass. I like that." He dipped his head and captured her mouth. Before they'd both gone at each other like starved animals. Now…well, now he wasn't any less hungry. If anything, he only wanted her more. But it was a banked hunger, allowing him to linger, savor, take his time. When he lifted his head, her eyes were shut, her lips curved in a satisfied smile.

He kicked off his trousers completely, gathered her close and stood. Her eyes flew open, then she merely looped her arms around his neck and lay her cheek against his chest. "See, I knew you were a sweeper."

He headed toward the bedroom he could see beyond an open doorway. "Apparently, with you, I'm many things I've never been before." He didn't glance down, didn't want to see the questions form in her eyes. He wasn't quite ready to risk giving voice to the answers. Not just yet.

He stopped in front of the doors leading to the two bathrooms. One held a sauna and a separate glass-enclosed shower, the other a whirlpool tub. "Sauna or hot tub?"

"A shower will be steamy enough, don't you think?"

He stepped into the "His" bathroom and let her slip from his arms, keeping her body close as her feet touched the inlaid marble floor. With her arms still twined around his neck, he backed her into the roomy shower stall and flipped on the water. He tucked her into the corner, taking the brunt of the cold spray which rained down from the multiple fat shower heads on his back. It only took seconds for the water to warm up and the steam to begin to rise.

Along with something else.

"Do you always shower with your clothes on?" she asked calmly.

"What clothes?" he murmured, kissing the side of her neck, letting the hot water sluice over them both.

"Your shirt..."

He dragged the unbuttoned shirt down his arms and let it drop with a wet *thwap*, never taking his lips from some part of her anatomy. "I suppose you'd like to take this skirt off then?" he asked, kneeling in front of her. She managed a nod, arched as he reached behind her to slide the zipper down. He had to tug a bit, the wet material clingy and tight, to get it past her hips. He wasn't in a hurry as his mouth was busy lapping up the rivulets of water tracking down her stomach, into her navel, then back out again.

When he dipped his head, lapped even lower, she braced her hands on his shoulders. "Tucker...dear God," she breathed.

"Just what I was thinking," he murmured, wondering if he'd ever have enough of her. Probably not, he imagined as she began to pump her hips against his seeking tongue.

He slid his hands up her slick belly, found her nipples hard and begging for his fingertips to massage warm water around them.

Her nails dug into his shoulders and the light sting only aroused him further. He continued to play with her, tease her with his tongue, until she quivered beneath his touch and the hot spray of water.

"There," she gasped. "Right there. Stay...right... ahhhh, yes," she finished, moving to a guttural groan as she went over for him. Her knees buckled and he shifted up on his feet just in time to catch her and keep her from sliding down the wall. He draped her arms over his shoulders and braced her body against the wall with slight pressure from his. There was no way to disguise how aroused he was. Not that he bothered to try.

"Amazing," she managed.

"Funny," he said, nuzzling her neck. "I was thinking the same thing."

"That, too." She shifted her thighs, captured him between them. She nudged him aside, kissed his neck, lapped at the water that ran along his shoulder. He twitched hard at the feel of her soft tongue on him. "But I was referring to this." She squeezed her thighs.

The groan slipped out before he could stop it. "You don't have to—we don't—"

She opened her eyes then, framed his face with her hands so they looked at each other. "I have more sponges, but seeing as we're already in the shower...

and you're so…'' She squeezed her thighs again, then grinned when he tried to shift and she refused to let him.

"A little dominant streak in there after all?'' he said, thinking this was the kind of sweet torture he was willing to take.

"No, I just happen to believe in fair play.''

Before he could question just what she meant by that, she'd slithered from his grasp, and slid downward. Letting her tongue lead the way.

He didn't resist when she nudged him back beneath the spray until his back met the other wall. She cupped him, then slicked her hand down the full length of him. "So,'' she said, looking up at him, the water streaming down over her pale, perfect skin. "May I play?''

He could only nod. Then groan as she slipped her mouth over him and took him. He didn't last long, was surprised he'd peaked at all considering he'd just come not a half hour before. He was dragging her back up to her feet even as the brief climax was still rippling through his body.

"Tucker—''

"Shh, just come here.'' He pulled her into his arms, let her rest against his body, then reached up to angle the wide shower head so it drenched them both. "Just relax.'' She turned her face away from the spray, rested her cheek on his chest, one palm covering his heart, the other draped around his waist.

He stood there, holding her, feeling the perfection of how she fitted so naturally against him, so wonderfully. He let the water beat down on them, and came to terms with the fact that, in the space of twenty-four hours, his life had been irrevocably altered.

And no matter what he told himself, postcoital lust had nothing to do with this. The woman in his arms did. And he never wanted to let her go. It was as simple, and as God almighty complicated as that. What he didn't know was what in the hell to do about it. About her. About keeping her right here, where she was meant to be.

PRESSED AGAINST his slick chest, the steam enveloping them both in a blissful cloud of heat and relaxation, Misty let herself drift. He was so sturdy, so perfect, holding her as if he meant to do so always. And wouldn't that be wonderful, she told herself dreamily. To have Tucker. Simply have him. Here. There. Everywhere.

The sex. It was the sex, she thought, lethargy seeping into every pore along with the water. Stupendous sex, she appended. She'd never been so in tune, so comfortable, taking, giving, playing, with anyone. Of course, she'd known it could be like this. In fiction, anyway. And now that she'd found it for real? Well, who wouldn't want that forever and always?

Those broad hands stroking her back, the steady beat of his heart beneath her fingertips. Steady. Sturdy. Stalwart, she thought, a sleepy smile curving her lips. He was all that and more whether he wanted to believe it or not. And for the moment, all that was hers.

At some point as she drifted, he slicked soap over

her shoulders and back, shampoo was massaged into her scalp. "I'm never letting you leave this room," she murmured, as he tipped her head back so the spray could rinse her off.

"You won't get any argument from me."

"I suppose I should be nice and give you the wash and rinse treatment, too."

"I'm having a perfectly wonderful time, don't worry about me."

"Okay then," she said, eyes still shut as he shifted her around so her back rested on his chest. He soaped her breasts and belly…and more. "I'll just force myself to allow you to do what you will." She glanced up and cracked one eye open. "All in the name of being fair, of course."

"Of course," he said, quite caught up in sliding his body down hers, running soap-slicked hands along her thighs and down over her calves. He straightened and pulled her close again. "All clean," he said, pressing a kiss against her hair.

"Are you sure you didn't miss any nooks or crannies?"

He pushed the shower head away and tipped her face to his. "I don't think so. Would you like me to check again? As an investigator, I believe in being very thorough."

"Yes, I believe I already know that about you."

He reached behind her and shut the water off.

"Wait, what about you?"

"I used you as a body sponge," he said with a wicked grin. "I'm squeaky."

She ran a finger down the center of his chest. "So you are."

He popped open the shower door and reached for the towels. She finally mustered up the energy to move and beat him to it. "You washed, I dry."

He grinned. "I thought that only applied to dinner dishes."

She slipped the towel off the rack. "Aren't you the clever one. Now, do you want me to dry or not?"

In reply, he stepped onto the mat and held his arms out. It was her first time really getting a full-length look at him. Dear God, he looked as good as he felt. Better even. Smooth skin, all burnished gold, defined muscles. Imagine that, she thought. She'd come to Las Vegas and hit the jackpot without ever entering a casino. *Well done, old girl.*

"Am I on the air dry cycle here?" he teased, obviously not minding her staring in the least.

She laughed and began to pat him dry.

"I'm not fragile."

"I'll agree with that." She patted and rubbed until he looked like a buffed god. Made her want to lick her lips. So she did.

He caught her at it and winked. "My turn." He snatched the towel from her before she could stop him.

"I'm quite capable—"

"I believe we've covered that. Now, turn around."

She did a pirouette, then curtsied.

"Very funny. And quite lovely. Dance lessons?"

"Miss Pottingham's School of Charm and Grace."

He paused in drying her arms. "You're not making that up, are you."

She shook her head, then sniffed and struck a snooty pose. "I'll have you know you're presently drying off one of Miss Pottingham's greatest achievements. If my parents are to be believed, at any rate."

"Born with a silver spoon in your mouth, were you?"

"Oh darling, I had the entire tea service. Yet, I was most often found getting into mischief with the stable lads and the staff offspring, or up a tree in the orchards, reading this book or that." She smiled and snatched the towel back from him, wrapping it around her. "Much to my parents' eternal dismay, I was always rather hoydenish. It was a minor miracle to get me to sit at the piano, much less put on a proper dress."

"I can see where a shrine, or perhaps a simple marble statue, should be erected in Miss Pottingham's honor then." Tucker followed her from the steamy room, apparently quite comfortable dressed only in his own skin. As it happened, Misty was quite comfortable with his chosen outfit as well.

An instant later he surprised a squeal out of her as she found herself airborne momentarily, before landing on the wide blue ocean of bedspread. Tucker landed, graceful as a cat, just behind her, rolling her, now breathless with laughter, onto her back and pinning her effortlessly to the bed.

"I think you still like to get into mischief," he said.

She stared up into those dark, devilish eyes of his, prepared to toss back a witty rejoinder. What came out was far more sincere and heartfelt. "Actually, I think I'd forgotten all about how to play for the sheer fun of it." She reached up and stroked his cheek, then ran her finger across his bottom lip.

He captured it and pulled it into his mouth, eyes on hers the whole time.

"Until today," she finished. "You make it quite easy."

He released her finger, dropping a quick kiss to her palm before her hand moved away. "You're never too old to play. How else are you going to tell when you're not working?"

She grinned up at him. "Good point. Perhaps it's because my work is mostly in my head. I carry my office around with me, so to speak, so I can never leave it."

"So," he asked, trailing blunt fingertips down her arms, making her damp skin tingle. "Have you been thinking about work the past couple of hours?"

"Not once, actually." She wriggled when he hit a ticklish spot. "I never mix business with pleasure."

He caught her gaze. "Even though pleasure is your business?"

She stilled then. She'd thought he was teasing her, but now realized there was another question lurking beneath the surface. "If you're asking me if you're research for a book, the answer is no." *You're just for me,* she wanted to say. *All for me.* "As I said, I don't mix business with...anything." She went to pull away, but his grip on her wrists tightened.

"I'm sorry. I'm sorry," he repeated when she turned her face away from his. "I deserved that."

"Yes, you did."

"Look at me."

She thought about resisting him, but truth was, she didn't want to. She looked up at him, said nothing.

"I believe in play," he said. "In having a good time when the opportunity presents itself." He shifted, trapping her when she went to pull away again. "I also believe that anything is possible. Today…this time…with you…" He drifted off, simply stared down at her.

She didn't know what it was she saw in the depths of his eyes. Confusion. Wonder. Desire. Maybe all three. Maybe more.

"It started out as an opportunity, one I couldn't pass up," he said. "I wanted to be with you, haven't stopped thinking about you since we met. I wanted to have fun. And now…" Again, he didn't finish.

"And now what?" she finally asked, her voice barely a whisper. Her heart tripped, doubled its rate, then stuttered again. What did she want him to say? That there could be more?

"I know we agreed on no boundaries, but they're there. And I find myself already pushing up against them. It might not seem fair, but I guess I want to know I'm not only a good time, a means to an end."

She didn't respond right away. If she had, she might have blurted out things best left for midnight fantasies, when he was nothing but a memory. "You are a good time," she said carefully. "But I'm not using you as some sort of research project. Unless that project is me."

"Misty—"

She had no idea what he'd been about to say, but she instinctively cut him off, unwilling to take the risk. The risk that it might be something that would ruin what they could have. Which was four days. Or maybe it was the risk that he'd say something that would make her confront the fact that four days might not be enough. For either of them. And she had no idea what to do with that. So she avoided it with a kiss.

"I came here wanting to learn more about myself," she said quietly, her lips still so close to his. "About my sexuality, my needs, fulfilling desires I'd only dared to try on paper. I didn't want complications that come with forging a relationship, because, frankly, up to now that was always a hindrance to fulfilling my desires rather than a boon. And Blackstone's offered me that opportunity. Then reality struck and that poor woman was murdered. One door opened, one door closed."

She watched him, wishing like hell she knew what was going on behind those impenetrable eyes of his. "And then I met you. And another door opened." She slipped her hands from his grasp, framed his face with her palms. "I'm not expecting you to fill those gaps. That's up to me. What we do is about us, between us, not about my work. This is about you telling me you wanted to spend time with me. And me realizing I wanted the same thing. That's why I stayed, why I came to your hotel. Why we're here, like this. I wasn't expecting anything more."

His eyes darkened then, and she felt a shiver of awareness course through her. Primal, she thought.

That's what he was. And that part of him touched something similar in her, some inner ferocity she hadn't known she possessed. Or perhaps she had but, unsure what to do with it, she'd channeled it into something she could deal with. Fiction, which had no boundaries, where she could do anything, be anything.

Most especially all the inappropriate things a well-bred Smythe-Davies would certainly never do.

Tucker touched her face, her mouth, looked as if he were about to say something, then instead lowered his lips to hers, took her in a kiss that was only gentle for a split second, before it became something fierce, something almost…savage. Possessive.

And she was swept up in it, those same feelings rushing through her, fueling her desire, her desire for him. Only him, she thought distantly, sinking her fingers into his thick, dark hair, clawing at his scalp, wanting to devour him whole.

He rolled to his back, taking her with him. She straddled him easily, only dimly able to wonder where this boundless appetite for him came from. She should be empty now, totally sated, exhausted of all needs and wants. But no, there was a hunger for him she hadn't even touched. And she was fairly certain, that even if she had him unrelentingly, for every moment of the next four days, she'd still be hungry when he left her.

Left her. Alone. She couldn't even think it. Not now, when she could immerse herself in him and all the emotions he churned up inside her. If only they were exclusively sexual. But they weren't. And there was the risk she faced. Feeding that hunger, while trying not to feed those deeper, profound needs she now realized were at the core of what she really wanted.

That need to belong, the one she'd felt in the shower, curled against his slick chest, tucked beneath hands that would shelter her, care for her. Protect her.

She, who had always protected herself.

Yeah, came that inner, taunting voice, *by running.* Hiding inside books.

She'd come here, hadn't she? some part of her mind fought back, even as she plunged her tongue into his mouth, mated fiercely with his, dominating, before he turned the tables and took over. *She was taking, wasn't she? Doing what she wanted, going after what she wanted? She wasn't running now.*

Tucker rolled her again, broke free, panting hard as he rose above her looking for all the world like one of his warrior ancestors. "What if I want more?" He said it as if the words had been torn from him, his voice a hoarse growl. He leaned in, gripped her head, held her there, his face merely an inch from hers. "What if I want more?"

Her heart pounded so hard, it should have drowned out every taunting thought. But it didn't. *Okay then, if you're not running, now what?* "Then maybe we take more."

She hadn't known what to brace for, but it wasn't the wild grin that creased his face, almost as untamed as the gleam in his eye.

"I don't think you'd have done well at Miss Pottingham's," she said faintly, her lips curving as a dangerous rush poured through her. Dear Lord, what had she done? What had she loosed? Both in him…and in herself?

"No?" he said, rolling between her thighs.

She shook her head, felt him nudging, miraculously, at her. "In fact, you would have been her downfall." *As you might well be mine.*

"I can't seem to get enough of you," he said, somewhat in shock himself as he pushed against her.

"I'm not complaining." Her body should be, but the only ache she felt was one of yearning. To be filled by him. Again. And again. "My—I need to—"

"Where are they?" he asked, understanding what she wanted.

"My bag. On the floor, by the bed."

He shifted, rolled off of her, making her pout without even being aware of it.

When he rolled back, he sported his own wicked grin…holding more than a small contraceptive package.

"And what are these for?"

Four lengths of black silken cord dripped from his fingers.

11

TUCKER HADN'T WANTED to leave her, even for a second. He just grinned when the cabbie eyed his damp, rumpled shirt.

"I let you out here?" the young man asked doubtfully.

"Yep," Tucker said, sliding out in front of his hotel after paying the fare. He smiled as the cabbie drove off, still shaking his head. So he looked a little disreputable. God knows he'd earned it. Thinking back on everything he and Misty had done in the past twelve or so hours he could only smile and shrug. Being insatiable was nothing to be ashamed of.

He ducked into the lobby, intent on getting a change of clothes, calling to cancel the remainder of his seminars, then heading back to the Bellagio. And Misty. If he was lucky, he could be back before she woke up.

His stomach rumbled loudly and he chuckled. Okay, so he'd stop and pick up some food on his way. Breakfast in bed. He punched the elevator button, already imagining just how he was going to wake her up...and exactly how he wanted his strawberries and cream.

"Tucker! Wait up."

He didn't even glance over his shoulder. Open, dammit, he silently begged the elevator doors. Then he could pretend that Mig wasn't headed his way.

Unfortunately, Mig jogged up to him just as the doors finally slid open.

"Hey, man, glad I caught you. I've been leaving messages since last night." Then he noticed the less than pristine state of Tucker's wardrobe and broke into a smile. "I guess you weren't here to pick them up, eh?"

"No," Tucker said, smiling despite wishing like hell Mig hadn't found him. He liked the guy, both personally and professionally, but at the moment he really didn't want him to be here. "In fact, I'm only here now to grab a change of clothes."

"Some night."

"You might say that."

Fortunately Mig was a better man than Strosnyder—but then, who wasn't?—and refrained from making an inappropriate comment that would have forced Tucker to plant his fist in his face.

"Any chance I can tear you away for a little while?" Mig asked. "We never got the chance to talk at the lab yesterday and there is something I'd really like your opinion on."

As much as Tucker wanted to get back to Misty, he was torn, if only for a second. "I don't know what I can offer you, man. I already told you my experience in your field is strictly classroom. And I thought you had Ralston cold?"

"So did we. But we got some new information in last night."

"The other lipstick?"

He nodded. "Doesn't match anything Ms. Denton had with her. But it does match the smear we found on the collar of Ralston's jacket."

He had Tucker's full attention now. "So Misty was right. He had someone with him. Or a girlfriend anyway."

"Looks that way."

"So, you've got premeditation now. It wasn't a crime of passion, maybe he just wanted her out of the way. First degree murder."

"Except we don't necessarily have the shooter."

"What?"

"We ran tests on Ralston's hands. No residue."

"So he was wearing gloves. Or he washed up well."

"Possible. We have no prints on the scene other than Ms. Denton and several employees. The thing is, Ralston defied his attorney and talked to us today. He's sticking to his claim that he wasn't there that night, says the driver is mistaken about who he saw at the gates. He also says he hasn't seen that jacket in weeks. Says he left it in his clubhouse restaurant and never got around to picking it up. We're checking with the waitstaff to see if anyone remembers seeing it recently."

"So anyone who picked up that jacket—"

Mig just nodded. "Now that lipstick is taking on a bit more importance. It's on the jacket, on the napkin, both of which were on scene."

"Even if Ralston might not have been."

"Exactly."

"He give you anything on a possible girlfriend?"

Mig laughed harshly. "Oh yeah, right. No, he claims he has no girlfriend, that he was faithful to his wife."

"His wife was a lot older than him, right?"

"Almost twenty years."

Tucker whistled. "So it wouldn't be a stretch for him to be out looking."

"Or for her to be getting her jollies elsewhere while he was."

"So, what do you need me for?"

"Conflicting results on the splatter analysis."

"Such as?"

"How tall the shooter was, for one."

Tucker laughed. "Hey, I was taking the analysis class from you, you know. You teacher, me student."

Mig smiled, but the look in his eyes remained serious. "At dinner the other night, you mentioned you took some courses on laser trajectory analysis."

Tucker had, and had been fascinated by the new development. They had special equipment now that shot thin beams of light from one location outward to every splatter point on a given surface. It revealed, amongst other things, a great deal about the exact position of both the shooter and the victim at the moment of impact. "Do you have the system?"

Mig shook his head. "And though I've wanted to take the training, I knew our budget wouldn't allow us to get the system anytime soon." He shrugged. "So I've put it off. So has everyone else. But we're working on borrowing one and if all goes well, we might have it here by tonight. You game in helping us set it up?''

''I'm not going to say no, but you know if Ralston's attorney wants to make a stink about you bringing me in on this—''

''This won't be pivotal trial evidence, but it will add another puzzle piece to the investigation. Whoever did this will be wrapped up so tight by the time we get done, there won't even be a trial.''

Tucker admired Mig's intensity, felt a tug of the same inside himself. ''I hope you're right.''

''Yeah. In the meantime, I'd like you to come in, look at the photographs, maybe take a look at the scene. So you'll know what to expect when the equipment gets here. I can wait for you to change, drive you myself.''

And that's when Tucker remembered where they were…and what he'd been planning to do this morning. And with who. ''Uh…damn.''

Mig grinned and this time it reached his eyes. ''Hell being torn between two lovers, isn't it? Main reason I've stayed single.''

Tucker chuckled and answered automatically. ''Yeah, well I don't plan on growing old alone.''

''Is that why you stay in that two-horse town of yours? So you can have your cake and eat it, too?''

''Maybe.'' Tucker had never acknowledged that before, but Mig had a good point. Canyon Springs was where a man married, raised a family, grew old, retired, went fishing with his grandkids. And where his job would never be so challenging that he couldn't have plenty of time to do it all. Had he always been so willing to settle for less, just in case?

"Not much variety in that cake though, I imagine." Mig grinned. "Either kind."

He was certainly right about that, Tucker thought. Misty was a whole new flavor. And Las Vegas a whole new bakery.

Mig studied him. "Looks to me like you're already enjoying sampling the variety life has to offer." He'd said it straight, no leer or offense intended.

"Sometimes life offers you the best slice when you least expect it," Tucker responded. "And where."

"We still talking about homicide?"

Tucker grinned. "Maybe."

"So, you need some time? I can send a car for you later. Can't promise Ted won't be driving it, though."

Tucker and Mig shared a look of disgust. "Let me go up and change, make a few calls," Tucker said. "Can you give me fifteen?"

"Sure."

Tucker took the next available elevator, wondering as he rode to his floor how a person's life could change so completely in such a short span of time.

He was already shrugging out of his clothes as the door to his room closed behind him. He grabbed a two-minute shower and pulled on fresh khakis and a dark blue polo shirt, smiling as he glanced at the rumpled heap of clothes on the floor. He wondered if Misty was awake yet and crossed to the phone by the bed before he'd tucked in his shirt. Suddenly he had to hear her voice, had to know how she'd sound first thing in the morning. She picked up on the second ring.

"Hello?" Her tone was sharp, almost distracted.

Tucker smiled bemusedly. Not exactly the drowsy, sexually sated good morning he'd expected. "You sound pretty chipper."

"And here I thought I just sounded smug." She laughed warmly and he wanted badly to be next to her, touching her. "I got your note. I ordered up some breakfast. Want me to save you some?"

"Actually, that's why I'm calling."

"Uh-oh, that sounds ominous."

"Mig met me here, he's waiting downstairs. He wants me to come in and look over some evidence."

"Sounds mysterious and interesting. I thought they had this case sewn up, though."

Tucker liked it that she didn't pout or whine. Although he felt like doing both. "Apparently Ralston is standing by his claim that he wasn't there, that the jacket was planted in his trash."

"What about the lipstick?"

"It's not Denton's. And they found traces of the same lipstick on the jacket."

"Curiouser and curiouser. Hmm."

Tucker paused then. Her interest was definitely sincere, almost too sincere. In fact, he swore he heard wheels turning. "Just what were you doing when I called anyway?"

"Is my distraction that obvious?" She laughed. "I was taking down some notes, actually. Wishing I had my laptop."

"Notes? And here you told me I wasn't research."
He said it teasingly.

"Well, I would have thought you'd have filled my
dreams as perfectly as you filled me."

Tucker choked on a surprised little laugh. "I take
it I didn't, however. I'll have to work harder next
time."

"I'm not sure you could be. Any harder, I mean."

"I know what you mean." So did his body, which
she aroused so easily. "So, what *did* you dream
about?"

"Murder."

Now he laughed outright. "You know what fasci-
nates me?"

"What?"

"You. Your mind." *And how I can be so head over
heels when I just met you.* "So, what notes were you
taking?"

"I'm plotting my next novel, and I'm thinking
about adding a murder investigation. Nothing about
this case, of course. It just got the juices flowing, as
they say."

"I like that saying, as it happens. So, you're thinking of shifting to erotic suspense?"

"Oh, I rather like the sound of that," she murmured. "I hadn't actually thought to label it, but yes,
that would be the appropriate term, I imagine."

He heard the rustle of paper and could only grin as
she drifted off again. "Why don't we plan to meet
for lunch?" he offered. "I might have to go back in
this evening for a couple of hours, but then we can
have the rest of the night." She didn't respond right

away, so he waited a few moments. When all he heard was a pen scratching on paper, he said, ''I thought we might finally get around to using those silk cords I found yesterday.''

''What? Oh!'' She laughed. ''I'm sorry. I'm lost in my story here. Amazing how neatly you pulled me out, though.''

''I thought it was rather clever.''

''I thought you promised to leave the accent to me.''

''So I did,'' he said, making them both laugh. ''You rub off on me, I guess. I don't even know I'm doing it.''

''Funny, but I always knew exactly when you were doing it.''

''Are we still talking about my horrible accent?''

''Maybe.''

Tucker grinned. Maybe that was what had him so wrapped up, that for as different as they were, in some ways their minds worked in a far too similar way. ''So, do we have a date?''

''Lunch you said?''

''To start.''

''Only if you promise we can talk shop while we eat.''

''I'm all yours. Pick my brain, ravish my body, whatever you desire.''

''Just lunch will do. For now.'' She laughed when he made a pouting little sigh. ''We can meet up again when you're done for a late dinner, maybe a little bondage for dessert.''

''I—'' He stopped as that last part sank in, gave

him a wicked little zing. She really was the damnedest woman he'd ever met. He thought about what she'd said to Ted, about seducing her reader's minds along with their bodies. She'd done that to him. Effortlessly. "I think I might be able to work that in."

Now there was no doubting the wicked ring to her laugh. "Oh darling, I'm rather counting on that."

The zing turned to a spike. He should be hobbling by now, considering all they'd done to each other the day before. But here he was, ready and raring to go. Again. He wondered how much time they'd have to spend together before that insatiable need wore off. And hoped like hell he'd get the chance to find out. "Well then, consider it done."

"Consider it considered. And Tucker, just so you understand, I didn't bring those cords for me."

Tucker was still trying to claw his tongue out of his throat as the dial tone echoed in his ear. He sat there for several long moments, thinking only an idiot wouldn't cancel everything and rush immediately back to her side. Except she was working. And Mig was waiting. And where she was concerned, there was something to be said for anticipation.

He finished dressing and made it to the elevator banks in time to snag a ride down without waiting. It was only as he descended to the lobby that he realized his anticipation was as much for lunch and shop talk as it was for their dinner. And bondage dessert.

Four days was definitely not going to do it. He was going to have to find a way to continue seeing her. How, he had no idea. But he still had a couple of days to come up with a plan.

Mig stood up as he entered the lobby. "All set?"

"Yep. One request though," he said as the idea hit him. "Is there a bookstore around here somewhere we could stop by?"

From the look on his face, Mig knew exactly whose books he was going to be hunting down. He grinned and shook his head. "You're a goner. You know that."

Tucker shrugged, but his grin was wide and he didn't bother hiding it. In fact, he wanted to shout it to the whole world. "Apparently."

Mig just laughed. "We've been trying to con you to stay here since you walked into our classroom and she gets to you in a few hours. Maybe we should get her to talk you into it."

Tucker just shot him a grin. "You know, being a goner isn't so bad. Feels pretty good. Damn good, in fact. You should think about trying it."

Mig shook his head. "Not me, buddy boy." He pushed through the lobby door. "Too much cake out there waiting to be sampled."

Tucker shrugged and said, "Well, I guess not all of us can find our own personal bakery."

Mig chuckled as they slid into his car. "How true, how true." Then he shook his head as he pulled out into traffic and muttered, "Lucky bastard."

Tucker thought that pretty well summed up how he felt at the moment. Fascinating work to be done and an even more fascinating woman to go home to. It didn't get much better than that. So maybe the time had finally come for him to put up or shut up. Pursue the job lead here. Leave Canyon Springs behind. Go after what he wanted instead of waiting for it to come to him. But what about Misty? How did he make that work?

"Whenever you get done daydreaming, we've got a case to discuss."

Tucker glanced over at Mig. "Hey, I'm just an unpaid consultant here. You only get to badger the hired help."

Mig shot him a look. "We're trying to arrange that."

Tucker looked back out at the passing city landscape, realizing the decision had already been made. He'd make it all work. Somehow. "Well, I might let you."

Mig slapped his thigh and chuckled. "Got ya."

Tucker let his grin widen, but kept his eyes on the scenery. "Looks that way."

MISTY WAS SITTING in a restaurant in Tucker's hotel, scribbling notes, when he pulled out the chair across from her.

"Sorry, I know I'm a bit late."

"No problem." She didn't look up right away, wanting to get her complete train of thought transcribed to paper first. To Tucker's credit, he didn't interrupt her, waiting patiently until she was done. She slapped the pen on her notebook and looked up at him. If she hadn't already felt a bit breathless with the incredible flow of creativity pouring through her, one look at him would have done it. "The hell with lunch," she said, enjoying that she didn't have to censor herself with him, in thought or deed, "I'll just eat you."

He responded with a grin that only served to sharpen her hunger.

"Maybe we should have called for room service rather than eat down here in the restaurant," she said.

"We keep trying to eat out. One of these days we might make it through an entire meal before we need some privacy."

Misty smiled and flipped her notebook shut. "Or semi-privacy, as the case may be. But no stairwells today."

Tucker pretended to pout. "What about car sex?"

"You don't have a car. And I draw the line with taxis. Besides," she reminded him, "you said you didn't want to mess around with me in public transportation."

"But cars are okay?" He tapped his chin in contemplation. "What about limos? With tinted windows."

"Only if that includes the one between driver and passengers."

"Spoilsport."

She shrugged, unrepentant. "I am spoiled. I don't like to share."

"And yet, who pulled who into the stairwell?"

"Ah, the chance of discovery is entirely different than having a built-in audience. And it's whom."

"Writers."

"Can be such a pain, I know."

"Funny, I only seem to recall the pleasure." He closed his eyes and groaned appreciatively.

Misty glanced around, but no one was paying them a bit of attention. Not that it would have mattered. Not with Tucker. Something about him, about the way he took care with her, and yet whose desire for her seemed almost uncontrollable...it was a potent combination. She found she trusted him, even as the edge they danced on every time they were with each other got sharper and sharper.

"Well, in exchange for picking on your grammar, you can dazzle me with your investigative prowess. I have some questions."

"And here I thought it was my *other* prowess you were dazzled with."

She could have told him quite honestly that she was as attracted to his mind as she was to his body. But seeing as he knew just how attracted to his body she was, that could be a dangerous admission to make. "I plan to make good use of both," she said, a sly smile curving her lips. "Unless you have any objections."

He raised his hands. "None at all." He folded his elbows on the table and leaned forward, motioning to her notebook with his chin. "So, I see the wheels have been spinning furiously while I've been gone."

She beamed. She couldn't help it. There was nothing quite like the rush that came when a new story was coming together. "I haven't felt this excited in a long time."

"You were pretty excited last night."

She merely raised an eyebrow. "Ha ha. But I was referring to my work. I enjoy it, but as I said before, I've found it more difficult of late to find new inspiration.'' She laughed. ''I never thought it would be murder that would solve that particular problem.''

He reached for her hand, picked it up, toyed with her fingers. ''Sometimes the things we want the most show up in unexpected ways.''

She stilled then, focused on his direct gaze, the feel of his fingers brushing hers. It was all rather exquisite, and made her want to believe what she was reading into his words. She slid her hand away before she said something foolish. ''It certainly did this time,'' she responded, quite honestly.

Tucker seemed to take her cue and returned his attention to her notes. ''So, are you setting the crime in your book in Las Vegas?''

She nodded. ''And it will involve a resort something like Blackstone's, only entirely fictional.'' She smiled. ''I can take creative license that way.''

His grin made the corners of his eyes crinkle. ''And I think I can say your readers will thank you for it.''

''Can you now?''

Tucker lifted a small plastic bag onto the table. She hadn't noticed it when he'd arrived because she'd still been jotting down her thoughts. ''I believe I can, seeing as I am one now.'' He pulled out her most recent novel, *Hot House*; an oversized, slender paperback that featured a crush of white orchids with a string of black pearls nestled in the center. He flipped it open to a page near the beginning. ''I like Rosalie.''

Misty wasn't quite sure how she felt about this. She was proud of her work and never apologized for the frankness of her stories. She enjoyed the letters she got from her readers, enjoyed knowing she'd brought them pleasure, or just a few hours of escape. But that was all rather abstract. It was another thing entirely to be seated across a table from a man she'd been more intimate with than any other, knowing he'd read her words. Which, especially in the case of Rosalie, was like reading her personal journal.

And yet, wasn't that why she was with him? To explore those fantasies for real? Wasn't it easier if he knew, up front, what it was she desired?

Like he hasn't already figured that out, she thought, then tried not to smile. With Tucker, what she desired was pretty much anything he wanted to do with her…to her.

"I didn't mean to make you uncomfortable," he said, breaking the sudden silence. "I really enjoyed what I've read so far. You've made Rosalie someone to care about." He grinned. "I'm hoping she ends up with Del, though."

Surprised out of her thoughts, she glanced up at him. "Really? Why? He's obviously not the type who would be there for her in the long haul. He's strictly—"

"Short term? Someone for her to learn with, but not good enough to stay with?"

She propped her elbows on the table, rested her chin on folded hands. "I don't know about good enough. She doesn't think in those terms. But do you really think he'd stick around? He doesn't want that kind of commitment."

Tucker tugged her hands free, pulled them both across the table, tracing circles in her palms as he held her gaze. "Oh, I think he does. He just doesn't know it yet."

Misty felt her heart stutter. Surely he was talking about her book. About Del and Rosalie. Not about them.

"So, am I right?" he asked. "Does she end up with him?"

He was right, and gauging from where the page was turned, he'd made his assumption very early into the story. "You'll have to finish the story, find out." She managed a light smile. "That's what makes a story successful, when you have to keep turning the pages."

"Oh, I'll finish it. And the others."

"Others?"

"They had four of your titles in stock. I got them all."

She blushed, truly flattered. "Thank you. I'd have sent you copies, you know."

"And I would have appreciated it. But when I want something, I usually don't wait to go after it."

She felt her body tighten at the message she saw clearly signaled in his dark eyes. Surely she wasn't misreading any of this. She cleared her throat. "Why did you pick *Hot House* to start with?"

"I started reading while I was waiting in line." He shrugged and smiled. "I was hooked."

She flushed again. It was always wonderful to hear a person enjoyed the words she worked so hard to put together. But with Tucker, it was more than merely gratifying. It was personally satisfying. Deeply so. He'd become personal, intimate, with far more than her body. He'd made it clear last night that he wanted more. He'd even told her before this whole thing began that he was going to push...and that she was going to want him to. And he'd been right.

But how far did she want this to go?

Last night, he'd been on the verge of telling her what he was feeling, but then he'd found those cords. And they'd ended up laughing and teasing, their lovemaking more playful than serious. They'd fallen asleep and when she'd awoken, he'd been gone, leaving a note promising he'd return quickly.

Now, here they were, having lunch. Talking shop instead of sex. And she knew she wanted that much, to get to know him better, learn more about him. But most of all, she wanted to know what he'd meant last night.

More what?

"And I've added a few things to my 'want to try' list," Tucker added, flipping through the pages.

He was so damn sexy when his eyes flashed like that. Misty smiled, realizing that she didn't have to ask him to explain what "more" he wanted. All she had to do was keep taking the next step. They'd figure out where they were headed when they got there. "I'm almost afraid to ask."

"And I'm beginning to think you're really not afraid of much of anything." Before she could respond, he flipped to another page near the end and turned the book around, pointing to a paragraph with a blunt-tipped finger.

She didn't look down—she knew exactly what

went on at that point of the story—but rather up at him. "I thought you started on page one?"

"I did, after I bought it. I didn't say which page it was that got me hooked." He tapped the page. "You haven't tried this, have you?"

She felt an instantaneous spurt of heat between her legs as she envisioned Tucker doing to her what Del had been doing to Rosalie. She had to fight to keep from squirming. "No," she managed. "No, I haven't."

"Would you like to?"

She held his gaze, felt a delicious sliver of anticipation snake its way through her system, then slowly nodded.

His eyes flared and he snapped the book shut. "Me, too." He shoved his chair back, barely giving her time to snatch up her pad and pen before pulling her along behind him. He stopped short a step later, turning back to her so that their bodies came right up onto one another. "I do have one question, though. Do they have to be real pearls?"

12

THEY FOUND A GIFT SHOP in the hotel lobby that sold long strands of colorful beaded necklaces. "Any particular color you want?" Tucker asked her, a downright wicked gleam in his eye.

If she weren't so incredibly turned on, she might have been embarrassed. As it was, she just wanted him to buy the damn things so they could head upstairs to his room. And put them to use. She shook her head, then said, "The blue ones."

Tucker just laughed and scooped up several strands and took them to the counter. He tossed two skinny packs of peanuts along with them. At her look of inquiry, he said, "Sustenance."

She merely nodded as the clerk rang up their items. If the young man suspected what they intended to do with their purchases, he didn't show it. But then, Misty hadn't looked him in the eye, so she wasn't entirely sure.

By the time they finally paid and left the store, she was aching to start this next adventure. But when she headed in the direction of the elevators, Tucker tugged on her hand and pulled her toward the front revolving lobby doors instead.

"Where are we—?" She stopped short and gasped

as she spied what was idling by the curb. "You didn't. How did you—?"

Tucker waved the driver back into the car and bowed as he opened the back door of the sleek, black stretch limo himself.

"When did you arrange this?" Misty asked, stunned.

Tucker winked at the bell captain, who gave him a little nod and wave, then he helped her into the luxurious interior.

Misty swallowed her surprise and slid along what had to be a mile of soft black leather until she was on the far side of the car. Tucker climbed in behind her, his long legs making the roomy interior suddenly much more close and intimate.

A small center panel in the solid partition separating them from the driver slid open. "Where to, sir?"

"Just drive around town. We want to see the sights."

"Thank you, sir." And the panel whispered shut. A moment later the car pulled away from the curb.

Misty was still trying to gather her wits when Tucker opened a small console and pulled out a bottle of champagne. "Shall we?"

"It's only one o'clock in the afternoon."

"And?"

And she couldn't believe he'd managed all this. They'd gone straight from the restaurant to the gift shop. He'd only gone back to pick up his— "So that's when you arranged this. Mr. I-left-my-bag-by-the-table."

"I did leave my bag. The rest was sort of spur-of-the-moment.'' He slid closer, still holding the champagne bottle. ''We can just see the sights, Misty.''

She looked at him, thought about the purchase they just made, about the reason behind that purchase…and then scoped out the rather roomy interior. ''A small glass won't hurt.''

Tucker grinned and worked the cork until it popped. ''Oh, I wasn't thinking we'd use any glasses.''

She just squirmed in her seat.

''Come and get it,'' he taunted, then took a small swig from the bottle and pulled her head to his.

Misty kissed him, tasting the tart zing of the sparkling wine on his lips. She wanted more, so she slipped her tongue into his mouth, and enjoyed the rush of just how delectable a champagne Tucker kiss could be. The heady mix of wine along with the anticipation of what else he was offering her had her taking the kiss deeper, had her pushing him back along the leather seat. She straddled him and lifted the bottle from his hand. ''My turn.''

Tucker watched her as she took a sip from the bottle, then leaned in for a wet, warm champagne kiss of her own. He groaned as he pulled her deep into his mouth, but she was already moving away, tugging his shirt from his waistband with her free hand. He shifted, helped her, and the polo shirt was gone, leaving all that wonderful, smooth plane of his bared chest for her to do with what she pleased. And she pleased a great deal.

Another sip, only this time she leaned over and ran a fizzy-wet tongue around his nipple, then the other.

She was very gratified with his intake of breath, the way he tightened beneath her tongue, the way his hips began to move as she shifted her weight back and moved lower. Another sip, and this time she dipped her tongue into his navel.

"Dear God," he breathed.

She looked up at him, all innocence and wonder. "Is this what you had in mind?"

"Actually, I thought I'd be the one—" He broke off when she slipped his belt loose and unfastened the waistband of his khakis. "But I'm all for spontaneity," he finished, jaw clenched as she worked his pants and briefs down along his hips.

Another sip, then a sharp gasp from him as she took him into her chilled, fizz-filled mouth. He bucked hard against her, but she kept him inside her mouth, enjoying immensely the feel of him growing even harder as she worked her tongue around him. Immense being a key word in more than one way.

She released him, much to his vocal dismay, then tucked the bottle in the convenient little holder in the center console...and picked up the gift shop bag.

Tucker managed to open his eyes at that point, but he said nothing. Watching her with a glittering dark gaze as she slipped out one long strand of gold beads and let the rest fall to the floor, still inside the bag. Straddling his calves she slipped the beads through her fingers...and licked her lips. Tucker's visible shudder made her feel downright invincible. "This is quite lovely you know, seeing the sights. I'm certainly enjoying them," she said, running her gaze slowly over every inch of him. Some inches more than once.

"Yeah." His voice was taut, hoarse. He throbbed and twitched as she continued to slip the beads from one palm to another. "Best idea I've ever had."

They were in their own private little world, the real one blocked out with tinted windows and privacy screens…and yet the thrum of the city was right outside. She hadn't forgotten that. In fact, the very idea made this entire escapade that much more thrilling. Which she assumed was exactly what he had in mind. However, and she grinned quite wickedly as she thought this, she was fairly certain he hadn't expected her to take charge. Which was what made doing so all the more fun.

Her heroines always took charge…in their day-to-day lives. Which was why, when she got them into the hands of their lovers, invariably taking charge was the last thing she allowed them. It was precisely that element of pleasure that she'd wanted to experience at Blackstone's. Men never minded when you took charge, but it was another matter entirely to trust them with taking complete charge of you. And she meant complete. And trust was only part of it.

She let the beads slither onto Tucker's chest in a cool pool of gold, then dragged them lightly over his nipples, then down lower.

However, with Tucker…she imagined he had no trouble taking charge. And she already knew she'd allow him almost any liberty with her. In fact, she craved it. But given his surprised reaction, she didn't imagine he found himself in this position very often. Which made her all the more determined to see that he stayed in it for as long as she could manage it.

She wanted him delirious with pleasure. And this way they'd both get a brand-new experience.

She slid the beads again from palm to palm as an idea took shape. A very specific shape. She had to smile.

"Wicked woman," he ground out.

"I just realized that I didn't need lessons on what to do…I just need the proper motivation." She let the beads pool on his stomach, then dragged them lower. "And I'm quite motivated at the moment."

Tucker growled in appreciation.

She draped the beads around what was, by now, an impressive erection. She circled the beads slowly, alternating watching how the gold glittered against his dark skin, and how darkly his eyes glittered as he watched her. She wasn't sure which made her wetter.

When she'd coiled the entire length around him, she wrapped her hand around the beads to keep them in place, then slowly, gently, ran her hand up and down along the beads, moving them in a rippling motion over his tight velvet skin.

"Jesus," he panted, but he left her to do what she wished, clenching his hands into fists by his head.

She was clenching tightly, too. She desperately wanted to feel him inside her, feel that velvety steel strength surging and—

She was panting now, too. Bending over, she began unwrapping the beads, replacing them with her lips as she continued to unravel him…in more ways than one.

"I want…inside you," he managed. "Now."

With a savoring last little lick, she released him

and sat back, amazed at how wonderfully sure of herself she felt, all powerful and incredibly wanton. She felt wickedly free when she unbuttoned the front of her loose cotton sundress, spilled out of her pale rose silk bra as she opened the front clasp. She let the bra slip through her fingers, let the sundress slide down her arms and off, then slid the strand of beads over her head. Slowly, she rolled them over her own nipples with her palms. It was when she tipped her head back and moaned at her own ministrations that Tucker's control snapped.

He gripped her hips, shoved her dress up, groaned when he discovered she wore nothing beneath. He all but plunged her down on top of him and they both moaned as he filled her in one hard thrust.

She was more than ready for him. Dear God, but no one could fill her the way he did. She fell forward, bracing her palms on his chest, only to have them yanked free as he tugged her the rest of the way down and took her mouth as fiercely as he was taking her body.

He held her head, plundered her mouth, wrapped his free arm around her waist, holding her where he wanted her, taking her, even from beneath, in powerful strokes.

It didn't take long before they were both careening out of control. She came first, with a shriek of delight that surely was heard by passing motorists. At that moment she could have been naked in the middle of downtown Vegas and she wouldn't have cared. Tucker climaxed right on the edge of hers, seemingly driven over the edge by her continued, shuddering demands of, "More! Yes, God yes!"

And when it was over, she lay completely and blessedly spent on top of him. Just how did a person recover, she wondered, and put their clothes back on and finish the ride with some modicum of dignity, pretending they hadn't been screwing their brains out. Only it wasn't like that, would never be with him, something she knew even before he proved it so.

He tipped her head to his, dropped an exquisitely perfect kiss on the tip of her nose, and said, "I definitely have to look into getting my own limo."

She propped her chin on his chest. "I believe I could become addicted to that particular form of pampering."

He searched her face. "I believe I could become addicted, too," he said quietly, then pulled her mouth to his and kissed her in a way that had nothing to do with sex and everything to do with that next step she'd been so worried about.

When she finally lifted her head, she knew she had a choice to make. Say something, take a chance that she was right about what he was feeling and tell him she was feeling the same way...or make a glib comment and keep them on their predetermined playpals fun track.

It was a palpable moment, one that felt as if it stretched on for days instead of seconds. Her heart pounded with the risk of it, the fear of changing things irrevocably. For the better or the worse. Things were pretty damn near perfect right now, so why say anything? Why this need to rush things along?

Three days, that's why. At some point, if she wanted more, she was going to have to say so. And waiting until she was boarding her plane didn't seem like a good idea.

"Wheels are turning," he murmured, stroking her face, then tapping lightly at her temple. "I assume you're not plotting your next book...so what are you plotting?"

The rest of my life?

She started to sit up, reach for her bra, thinking this wasn't a step she should take half-naked, but Tucker pulled her back down, nestling her easily along his body. She didn't fight him. It was, after all, exactly where she wanted to be. She laughed.

"What?"

"It's amazing, but I'm quite comfortable, sprawled atop you as we whisk about town."

"I'd like to think we'd always be comfortable wherever we are, just because we're together." He grinned then, as if to take the edge off his sudden sentimental bent, but the sincerity was there in his eyes.

So, instead of emotional proclamations, she simply said, "I'd like to think so, too." And when he kissed her, then tucked her hair behind her ears and smiled as if looking at her was all he needed to make him happy, she relaxed, knowing she'd handled it the right way. Apparently their relationship was going to progress whether they announced their feelings or not.

And even if she had no idea how to go about falling in love, she knew, somehow, he'd be there to help her figure that out, too.

She rested her cheek on his chest, settling her weight along his side and against the back of the seat while tracing lazy patterns on his chest and abdomen. "Why a fire investigator?" she asked at length.

"Hmm?" he responded drowsily.

She glanced up and found him, eyes shut, drifting peacefully, holding her close.

She could let him drift, but she wanted to know more about this man who was stealing her heart. Or maybe he was rescuing it. It was, after all, what he was good at.

"Your line of work," she reiterated, speaking softly, but determinedly. "How did you get into it? And how did that lead to the forensics you're doing here?"

He lifted his head, met her gaze with a questioning one, but when she simply smiled at him encouragingly, he let his head drop back to the seat and began to trace his own patterns along her spine as he spoke. "My father."

"He was a fireman?"

"No. He ran a grocery store. But he was a strong believer in giving back to the community. He'd been raised mostly on the reservation by his grandmother, had a strong sense of giving, forming bonds, helping. He was always helping those in need." He sighed, but it was a sound steeped in pleasant memories and Misty smiled, envying him. "I volunteered with the local rescue squad when I was in high school," he went on. "Because it was a way to help out." She felt his grin, heard it in his tone. "And a way to meet girls."

"Fancy that."

He shrugged, stroked her shoulder. "I believed in giving back to the community, too."

She looked up then. "Oh, I just bet you did."

The gleam in his eye was wicked. "We all do what we can."

Holding his gaze, she dipped her head slightly and swiped the tip of her tongue along his nipple. The flare in those eyes made her smile. "Why yes, I can understand that."

"I see you do."

She ducked her head, laid her cheek back on his chest before he could draw her back into the carnality that seemed to hover about them all the time. "So, when did the volunteering become a career?"

"The first time I rescued someone." There was a moment, a slight pause, and she felt his heartbeat speed up. "She was in her eighties and didn't want to leave her smoke-filled apartment without her cat. He was her only family."

Misty didn't say anything, just gently stroked his skin, letting the reality of what he'd chosen to do with his life sink in. It made her choices, her worries, seem so frivolous.

"I got her out. Then went back in for that damn cat."

Her throat tightened and she pressed a kiss over his heart. "You shouldn't have." She looked up at him. "But I bet you saved him, too."

He looked at her, a thousand memories in those dark eyes of his, and she was certain not all of them had a happy ending. "Yeah. Yeah, I did."

She pressed a kiss to his lips. A kiss of promise, a promise that while he was always there to help others, she'd be there for him. It was a promise she had no idea if he'd let her keep, but she made it nonetheless.

He kissed her back, and it deepened, into something of a promise for them both.

When she lifted her head, looked into his eyes, it was right there on the tip of her tongue, to tell him she was falling. But she ducked her head, let the moment pass. "When did you begin investigating fires?"

His hold on her tightened. "Arsonist. Set a store on fire down the street from my dad's store. Killed a good friend of his. And we all knew who did it, but we couldn't prove it. So I started digging. Pushing. Learning. We didn't get him. He took off."

"But you've gotten many like him."

"Yeah." He pressed a kiss to the top of her head and sighed. "Yeah."

There was a palpable pause then, so she lifted her head. "What's wrong?"

He looked directly at her. "I'm thinking of relocating."

It should have surprised her, but it didn't. "Here?"

He nodded. "As a member of their forensic investigation team. I'd need some additional training, but Mig is looking into that for me. Fire marshals, at least in my county, have to complete the police academy just like any other law enforcement officer, so I'm not that far behind." A wry smile quirked the corners of his mouth. "Sheriff Jackson back home is going to love this."

"What about you?" She sensed both his excitement at the opportunity...and his ambivalence.

"Dylan has been pushing me in this direction almost from the moment he left the force here." At her look, he said, "We grew up together. I was the gridiron hero, he was the town bad boy. We've had what you might call a friendly rivalry ever since. He left for the Vegas police force the day he was of age, but came back a few years ago." He toyed with her hair. "I guess it was the right thing for him. He likes his job, even got married a little while ago. Bad boy settles down and all that." He laughed. "Although with a wife like Liza, I'm not sure 'settled' is the right term." His grin faded to a wistful smile.

"And here you thought you'd be the one to settle down, be the town leader, is that it?"

He glanced up into her eyes, smiled. "Think you're pretty clever, do you?"

"We writers are an observant lot."

He tugged on a strand of hair. "I'm getting that. And you'd be right, in this case. Home, community, they've always meant a lot to me. It's not that I haven't thought about leaving, I have."

She heard the "often" without him having to say it. "So why haven't you?"

"I guess I always saw myself having what my parents had. Raising a family, working as a team, with each other, with the community. Canyon Springs is perfect for that."

"That doesn't mean you can't do that somewhere else. I'm sure a lot of the guys on the force here have families."

"I'm sure you're right. I guess I just pictured what I pictured, you know? Hard to realign that image."

"Will your parents be upset with you leaving?"

He shook his head. "They're both gone now."

"So why now? Did Mig persuade you?"

"Oh, they haven't been shy about nudging me and I know they'll do everything they can to help me make the transition. And I appreciate that." He looked at her. "Since coming here, things have happened that I didn't count on. I guess I realized that not everything happens the way you plan, and maybe instead of clinging stubbornly to what I thought I had to have, the way I thought I had to have it, I should look at what I really want and go after it. Maybe the rest will follow, I don't know. But I have to try. Waiting around for it isn't working." He continued to look at her, and she swore he was going to say something else, but in the end he just grinned and tucked her back against his chest. "So, your turn. Why did you become a writer?"

She had a hundred other questions, not the least of which was finding out if a new job was all he wanted, but fair was fair. She laughed dryly. "For the exact opposite reason you became a firefighter. You wanted to belong, I wanted to escape."

"Your family isn't proud of their accomplished daughter?"

"In their own way, perhaps. Their friends all know what I do for a living, but it's certainly not something one discusses in public, if you know what I mean." She knew her accent was sharpening, refining to a cutting edge. She worked to soften it. Tucker already understood her far too well and she didn't want any tension marring what had, so far, been a lovely interlude. "You see, whereas you were raised to bond and commune with your fellow neighbors, I was raised to be a credit to my family by being well educated, well mannered and well married. In that way I would bring honor and prestige to the Smythe-Davies heritage, and perhaps added wealth if I was savvy enough to bag a rich one. I was certainly never to consider doing anything that would bring shame or notoriety." She gave an exaggerated shudder. "Oh, the horror of it all."

"Ah."

She giggled at the wealth of emotion he'd put in that one syllable. "Exactly."

"When did you come to America?"

"I'd just graduated university with a degree in art history and my family was well into planning my wedding."

"Being a good girl to the bitter end and all that rot?"

She lifted her head. "Quite. And your accent hasn't improved one whit."

He grinned unabashedly. "So, who was the fortunate young man?"

She frowned, then sighed a bit sadly.

"I'm sorry, I didn't mean to make fun."

"No, it's not that. I have no regrets. It was no love match, we were all but betrothed before I was wearing my first bra." Her lips twisted into a dry smile. "Which was shortly before he asked to borrow it."

Tucker sputtered and tried not to laugh.

She lifted her head. "No, go ahead, it's quite alright and every bit that ridiculous."

"Did they know? Your family?"

"Oh yes, everyone knew. James didn't work overly hard at concealing his sexual orientation. But you see, that wasn't the point. Joining our family pedigree to his, looking good for society, that was important. Everyone knew, without ever speaking of it, of course, just as they assumed we'd have an understanding, as it were. We'd be quite free to lead our own lives, seek our own pleasures, as long as we put on the proper face. And joined the family accounts. They see nothing hypocritical about this. That's the part that amazed me."

"It's not amazing, it's awful."

Now it was her turn to sigh. "I know. I thought the same thing. James was quite willing to see it through, however, as it kept him in his inheritance. And in my narrow little worldview, I couldn't see any other way, so I agreed. And I honestly thought I could go through with it, stuff away my dreams and become what I'd been raised to be."

"So, why didn't you?"

She propped her chin on her hands and stared ahead, unseeing. "It was our wedding day." She glanced at him. "Apparently my inner hoyden wasn't sufficiently suffocated at Miss Pottingham's after all."

"You left him at the altar?"

She nodded. "I am that awful and that clichéd. I don't know which is worse."

Tucker laughed. "I don't know, better to duck out

five minutes before saying 'I do' than five minutes after.''

"Perhaps. But it took standing there, seeing all those faces, all the fake well-wishes and pretended nuptial bliss. I simply couldn't go through with the charade. I left the chapel, snatched what I could from my trousseau— Yes,'' she broke in sardonically, ''we are still that Victorian—and my passport and hopped a cab to Heathrow. I looked at the outbound flights and saw one for New York City. I thought that sounded like a place where I could simply lose myself, figure out what I wanted. And if I didn't like it, I'd find a place I did.''

"I can see where your heroine's get their grit.''

She smiled at that. "I think that's the nicest thing anyone has ever said about me.'' She laughed. ''But I felt more coward than heroine that day, I tell you. I was running.''

"Yeah, but that's not so bad when you're running toward what you want, is it?''

She looked at him. "You know, I never thought of it that way.''

He pulled her close then, so he could drop a lingering kiss on her lips. "So,'' he murmured, keeping her mouth close to his. ''Did you get the flat in SoHo, become a starving artist?''

She did laugh then. "Oh, nothing so noble as that. I landed a job in an art gallery, imagined myself falling in love with a starving artist, toiling away at making him a star by day while he gave me multiple orgasms in his loft every night.''

"I take it things didn't go as planned?''

"Um, no. To put it mildly. Pretentious pricks, most of them," she announced, making him laugh. She shrugged. "The ones I dealt with anyway. Self-absorbed and generally having no idea that life exists beyond their own little existential plane."

He was smiling with such wonderful affection as he looked at her, listened to her, she could have hugged him for it. "That sounded horribly bitchy," she said.

"But probably accurate. So, how did the writing start?"

"Oh, I'd always kept journals, writing down every flight of fancy I had." She shot him a saucy grin. "And you can't imagine how naughty I was on paper."

Tucker cupped her hips to his and wiggled. "Oh, I think I have a pretty good idea."

She laughed and nipped at his lower lip. "Yes, well, I wrote all the time in my little New York apartment. And the journals became fantasies, the fantasies stories. It helped me deal with the loneliness of a new city, the lingering guilt of leaving my family and James like that, not that I had any real regrets. I just wished it could have been done a bit more smoothly." She smiled. "And less publicly. It was writing that helped sustain me, my ideals, my decision to be my own woman."

"How did your journals go from the privacy of your bedroom to the local bookstore?"

"It was a chance meeting with a client who happened to work for a small New York publishing house. To this day I don't know what made me confess to her that I was a writer, but I did. She urged me to send her something. And, one night, on the eve of what would have been my second anniversary with James…I popped something in the mail to her before I could chicken out. The rest, as they say, is history.''

Tucker took her chin and turned her face to his. ''They should be proud of you. Your family. You've made yourself into a success, doing something you enjoy, which is a double reward. It's their loss they can't enjoy that, enjoy your happiness.''

She didn't know what to say. She'd thought the very same thing herself, but it was hearing someone else put it into words that finally had her truly believing it. ''You are a knight, you know,'' she said, brushing the softest of kisses on his lips. ''Whether you want to believe it or not. And I'm glad you're going to do what you want to do with your life, instead of what you thought life should do with you. Don't you think your parents would have understood? That your friends will?''

''Probably. Yeah.'' He dropped one gentle kiss, then another, longer, deeper one, on her lips. ''I think you've got some shiny armor on there yourself.''

She grinned, inordinately pleased with the compliment. It was wonderful to think she could lend him the kind of support he so effortlessly supplied to her. ''We knights of the realm have to stick together, you know,'' she teased. It was that or give in to the need to reveal just how perilously close to being in love with him she'd become. A man she'd only just met. Maybe the poets were right, and the heart simply knew.

He trailed his fingertips up her spine, leaving a sizzling reminder in its wake of what they'd been doing a short time ago. "I've got your back if you've got mine," he said, eyes flashing with amusement…and desire.

"Do you now," she said, drifting easily back into a playful, sexual mood. "And what might your plans be for said back?"

In answer to that, he leaned out, pressed a button that opened the intercom to the front of the limo. "Driver, the Bellagio, please."

"Yes, sir."

"I thought we were going to your hotel," she said.

"That would be fine. Except there's a certain set of silk cords at your hotel that I need to complete my plan."

She shivered with anticipation. "And what plan might that be?" She could hear the tremble of excitement in her voice. From the grin on his face, so could he.

He reached down and snagged the bag containing the other strands of beads. "We never did get to put these to their intended use."

She shuddered hard. "I thought you had to go back to the lab tonight." No way did she want to get into something, only to have him remember he had to be elsewhere.

"The equipment won't be there till morning." He jingled the bag. "So we have all night. And I plan to use every minute of it."

Misty wanted more than all night. She wanted forever. A plan of her own began to form, one she could put into motion while he was out solving crime to-morrow.

But she'd deal with that when the morning came. Tucker was doing something wickedly interesting with his tongue and she couldn't think quite straight.

Sometimes, paybacks were heaven.

13

THERE WAS A MESSAGE waiting for Tucker by the time they retrieved their play toys from Misty's hotel, and got back to his. "Not as fancy as yours," he teased as he unlocked the door, "only one bathroom."

They both saw the blinking light on the phone at the same time.

"You should see what it is," she said, stopping beside him.

The limo ride had been exhilarating, to say the very least, but Tucker's thoughts were now exclusively on having Misty all to himself, in the privacy of his own room, for the rest of the day. And night. The last thing he wanted was an interruption. He pushed the door shut and turned so that his body blocked hers, then backed her up against the wall. "I don't want to talk to anybody but you until tomorrow morning."

She pressed her palms against his chest. "What if it's an emergency?"

"Nothing can be as urgent as the plans I have for you." *Or the fact that the time we have left together is running out.*

She shivered at the dark promise in his voice, which only spiked his desire higher. He hadn't missed how she'd reacted to his comment about having plans for the beads, the silk cords, back in the limo. She might have claimed she brought them to use on some-one else, might have enjoyed her ride on top in the back of that limo...but given the type of "package" she'd all but admitted to signing up for at Black-stone's...and how she'd reacted to him running the show in the stairwell, well, he suspected she'd envi-sioned those silk cords used on herself. He planned to find out.

"Be that as it may," she said, her voice catching as he took her hands, pinned them to the wall beside her head, "I'd rather you found out now, than when we're..."

The rest of her sentence was lost as he slid her hands higher and lined his hips up with hers, leaving no doubt as to how involved he intended to be in the plans he'd made.

It was ridiculous how aroused she got him, and how little it took to do it. A lightly spoken word, a sardonic smile, a haughty whisper...and he was all but drooling to have her naked and beneath him. Or on top of him, as the case may be. Only this time it was his turn to be on top. Both figuratively and lit-erally.

She also had a point. Dammit. Once he began his erotic campaign to take her as he believed she wished to be taken...the last thing he wanted was an inter-ruption. He dropped kisses along her jaw, beneath her ear, then nipped at the soft, white lobe. "Okay, but no matter what, we're not going anywhere."

She turned her head, caught his gaze...and nodded.

Looking into her eyes, leaving no doubt she was as aroused as he was, only stoked him further. Which was the only reason he went ahead with his plan, made his request. Or demand, as the case may be.

He leaned in, pressed his lips to her neck, then very explicitly said, "I want you to pull that desk chair to the center of the room and sit in it."

When her pupils flared and she trembled, he realized she wasn't the only one who wanted to pursue this fantasy. He'd never thought about this kind of role-playing, about dominating a woman, not like this anyway. If anything, especially given his day job, he'd want to be the one to give up control, let her have her way with him. What man wouldn't?

But the palpable tension that had grown between them since they'd entered the room had clearly only spiked higher in the silence that had followed his quietly given command. Now it was up to her. Did she want this particular fantasy realized? All she had to do was say no, and they'd play it however she wanted. She knew that his intention was only pleasure…for both of them.

He held her gaze. "This only goes as far as you want it to," he said, unnecessarily he knew, when she nodded tightly. It pleased him in some elemental way that he did, indeed, have her trust. Even in this, especially in this, most vulnerable of fantasies. He vowed he'd do everything in his power to protect that trust, even as he did his level best to give her exactly what she desired. "But I'm going to push until you say stop."

She shuddered in response to that promise…and so did he.

And after another moment of heart-pounding silence, he had his answer. She walked quietly over to the desk, and pulled out the chair. It had a high wood back, carved in an open swirling pattern. The seat was padded, the legs straight, thick and sturdy. She pulled it to the open area between the desk and the bed.

"Face the window," he instructed.

She paused, but said nothing as she turned the chair as he'd asked. The light streaming in through the sheer curtains filtered through her light cotton dress, outlining her long legs and narrow hips. She looked up, caught him staring, then looked back at the chair…and sat, facing away from him. She didn't seem to know what to do with her hands, but finally put them in her lap.

He stood there a moment longer, behind her, wondering for a split second if this was an insanely stupid game to be playing. He respected her, he didn't want to subjugate her. But as he crossed around the foot of the bed, brushing past her on his way to the blinking phone on the nightstand, he glanced down and saw her hands lay loose in her lap.

Not fisted, not scared, or even particularly worried. He saw her chest was rising and falling more rapidly than her calm repose would indicate. Then he looked at her face…and saw the excitement banked in those passionate violet eyes of hers…and realized this wasn't about subjugation. Much less fear of any kind. It was about suspense, about anticipation, about wondering what was going to happen next…and how exquisitely long he was going to draw things out. It was about giving up control, putting him completely in charge of their pleasure.

It was as heady as it was intimidating. And it was that fact that leveled the playing field. After all, all she had to do was follow. It was up to him to be what she needed him to be.

He picked up the phone, mind spinning as he punched the message button. He listened, quite distracted by the fact that there was a woman waiting very patiently behind him for his next command, as Mig explained that he'd need Tucker at the crime scene very early the next morning. He saved the message, then hung up, but didn't turn back around to face her. She'd placed more then her trust in him. He knew without asking that she'd never exposed herself like this, revealed the depth of her needs, her fantasies, to anyone else. "Why me?" he asked quietly.

Her very stillness told him she understood how important her answer was to him. After a long moment, she said, "Because you'll take care."

Her answer undid him. Because that was the most important thing to him. To take care with her, give her everything she'd ever wanted, everything she'd never had. He also knew that fulfilling her sexual fantasies was only the bare surface of what he suspected she wanted, needed. He wondered if she had any idea how much he'd like to give her. Or of the man he found he wanted to be for her. If only she'd let him.

But here was a place to start. And when it was over and this particular fantasy had been played out, then he'd start in on giving her the rest.

"Slip off your shoes," he said softly, but in a tone that brooked no argument.

She sat up straighter then, understanding his signal that the play had begun. She held his gaze levelly as she toed off her sandals. And he fought the smile that threatened. So, despite the quiver of excitement that visibly chased over her, despite the vulnerable position she'd placed herself in…she wasn't about to be some meek, mild follower of commands. Her direct gaze almost defied him to control her. He should have known, from what little he'd read of her work, that she'd make the game her own. The smallest of smiles flirted with the corners of her mouth, as if she was enjoying his realization that, despite their respective roles, they'd both work for what they wanted in this room tonight.

He allowed his grin to surface, then, pleased to see hers falter, aroused to see her pull the corner of her lower lip between her teeth, suddenly a tiny bit unsure. He tossed the bag with the beads and cords on the bed, watched as she twitched a little at the rattling sound the plastic made as it hit the soft bedspread so close to where she sat.

Her chest rose and fell at a rapid rate. He had to work to keep his even as he walked around the chair, looking at her, but not so much as brushing up against her. "Do you know how stunning you are?" he asked roughly.

She kept her gaze straight ahead. "No."

He moved behind the chair, dropped to a crouch so his mouth was close to her ear. He heard her soft intake of breath, but she didn't move, kept looking straight at the window. "You are. You totally captivate me."

She said nothing, kept her expression carefully blank.

He found he wanted—badly—to get a response from her. "No woman has ever aroused me like you have. I've spent the greater part of the last three days either hard as a rock with wanting you, or wondering how long it will be before I'm hard for you again."

There was a slight catch in her breath, that he only heard because his lips were so close to her throat. "And I never have to wait very long." He wanted to taste that sweet soft skin, as much as he'd ever wanted to taste anything, but first he wanted that response. He shifted to her other side, blew very gently against the curls that lay on her neck. "Unbutton your dress."

Her breath caught, held, then released in a slow, measured sound.

"Now," he said sharply, gratified when she twitched.

Still, she didn't look at him, didn't in any way indicate she was aware of his proximity to her, or that she was aroused by it. It ground against his control, which he knew was precisely why she did it.

Slowly, she lifted her hands, plucked open each button, taking her time, until the fabric fell open almost to her waist. She let her hands rest in her lap when she was done.

He reached around her, very lightly ran his fingertips over the nipples pressing against the rose-colored silk. "I can't wait to have these." She shuddered at his touch, a shaky breath escaping through clamped lips. Then it was his turn to twitch. And throb. "But I will have them."

She made an obvious effort to straighten, square her shoulders, but was careful not to brush against him. He smiled...and ran the tip of his tongue along the shell of her ear. "I will have your control. One way or the other." He reached for the bag, slid out one length of black silk rope. Kneeling behind the chair, he reached around with both arms, took her wrists, carefully, so as not to touch any other part of her, and pulled them behind the chair.

"Cross your wrists."

She paused, and he saw her squirm, very lightly in the chair. It made him want to squirm, too. And rip off his pants, free what she'd already made so hard it ached.

He wrapped the cord around her wrists, gently tying a knot so that the rope barely held her there without slipping off. It was enough, he knew.

He stood, a powerful rush moving undeniably through him as he looked down at her from his now towering vantage point. It shouldn't be such a turn on, he thought, fighting it. But it was all that, and more. Maybe because she was allowing him, rather than being forced...it was almost a greater capitulation.

He moved around so that he faced her. She didn't look up at him, staring through him instead. Still in control, he thought, despite their roles. Well, he'd see to that.

He knelt again, right in front of her bare legs. "I want to see you," he said, reaching for the front clasp of her bra. She couldn't stop him, which somehow made baring her all the more darkly thrilling, but she didn't look at him, didn't react when he freed her breasts, slowly sliding the silk across her nipples. They were pebble hard, the only sign she was aroused, though he had no doubt she was as wildly turned on as he was. Still, she controlled him.

"I crave the taste of you," he confessed, then slowly ran his tongue along his lower lip.

She said nothing.

He leaned in, extending his tongue toward one tightly budded nipple, but stopping the barest breath away from touching her with it. "Do you want me to taste you?" he murmured.

He glanced up in time to see her chin tremble, but her lips remained flat…and closed.

"The feel of your nipples under my tongue…I dream about that, about how responsive you are to my touch."

He could hear her breath grow more uneven.

Again he leaned in, blowing a warm breath across one nipple, then the other. "Tell me to taste you, Misty."

She chewed the corner of her lip again, but said nothing. Her breathing grew more ragged.

"I want to pull them into my mouth, lick them, suck them. It will make you wet for me. Make me want to taste more of you." He blew across her skin again. "Tell me to taste you, Misty." He leaned in, tongue extended.

She shifted, just slightly forward, a brief moan escaping her lips when he pulled back.

"Tell me."

She didn't look at him, but she was trembling now. He could almost feel her skin vibrating.

He started to pull away entirely, rock his weight back on his heels.

"Taste me," she said hoarsely, as if the words had been pulled from her. Still she kept her gaze straight ahead.

He grinned even as his body tightened. "That wasn't so hard, was it?"

Twin amethyst gemstones glittered as she stared straight ahead, lips pressed tightly together.

But he heard her breath hitch as he slowly, so slowly, leaned in again, tongue out. He flicked the tip over one nipple, making her gasp, then tore a moan from her when, with no warning, he greedily took the other one fully into his mouth. She bucked in the chair, sliding forward.

He immediately, regretfully, pulled away. It was just as well, he told himself, at this rate he'd come before they got much further. He reached for the bag, slid two cords out. "Spread your legs."

Now she looked at him. A quick dagger of a gaze before she pulled herself back under control again.

"One heel by each chair leg," he instructed her. "It will only separate your knees several inches."

She slowly slid her heels into position and he rose onto his knees, grinning wickedly. "But you're going to wish it was more."

She held his gaze this time, her eyes dark violet now, and taunting him, pulling at him. Making him want to be her every fantasy incarnate.

He looked away this time, looped the cord around her slender ankles, tying each one loosely, but effectively, to a chair leg. Then, without warning, he leaned in and again took her nipple into his mouth, flicking at it with his tongue, wrenching a surprised gasp of pleasure from her, and a throat-deep moan from him. He drew his tongue up between her breasts to her throat, where he felt the skin pulse. He flicked his tongue over that, too, loving that he was responsible for the rapid vibration he could actually taste.

He lifted his head, brought his mouth right up to hers, almost but not quite pressing his lips to hers. "Kiss me."

She leaned in only as much as it took to create contact, pressed her closed lips to his in the barest of whispers, then relaxed back again.

"That wasn't a kiss."

She looked at him, saying nothing.

"Kiss me."

This time when she leaned in, he gripped her head and held her there, so that the contact continued.

"Kiss me," he said against her closed lips.

He'd expected continued resistance, so when her tongue suddenly speared past his lips, went deep into his mouth, he was caught badly off guard. He responded instantly, instinctively, holding her tongue tightly inside his mouth, sliding his between her sweet lips before he realized how neatly she'd trapped him. He broke away and now it was he who was breathing raggedly.

He rocked back on his heels, gathering his control. But when he looked at her, he found her again looking straight ahead. A hot little smile curving her now wet lips. Wet from the taste of him.

"Be warned, I might ask to trade places after this. And I remember everything." He leaned in again, took her mouth, refused her any shred of control, then, just as she whimpered, he whispered against her lips, "You're far too good at this, Misty Fortune. But I promise you, I'll be better."

She did look at him then, the light in her eyes totally at odds with those kiss-swollen lips. Amidst the desire, the yearning...was joy. And an honest affection for him, that when mixed in with everything else bubbling and churning between them, was the final downfall of his heart.

And that's when he realized that while he could have her, and he would, repeatedly...just as she could have him and likely would when the tables turned, that what he truly wanted to conquer, to own...was the one thing he couldn't force her to give him. Her heart. "Misty, I—"

She glanced at him then, obviously surprised at the shift in his tone and he caught himself. *Finish what you both started.* There would be plenty of time for the rest later. There had to be. Because a few days in a Vegas hotel room, no matter how explosive, weren't going to be enough. A lifetime, on the other hand, might do it. And with that greater goal in mind, he got back down to business.

His grin as he rose to his knees was powered by far more than his need to fulfill this particular forbidden fantasy of hers. If he had his way, he'd be there to fulfill them all. Maybe help her discover a few new ones along the way.

He placed the flat of his palms on her knees…and slowly pushed upward, slowly revealing the soft pale skin of her thighs as he shoved her dress higher. "Watch me, Misty." He looked up to find her doing exactly that. "I want you to feel every inch of that skin. Under my fingers…under my tongue."

She shivered then and he drew his hands back down her legs…leaving the soft fabric of her dress behind. He skimmed his palms along the outside of her thighs, then down along her calves, then back up, cupping her knees.

"Which do you want first?"

When she didn't answer, he reached up and toyed with one nipple, still damp from his mouth. She gasped and twitched in her seat. But didn't say anything.

"Fingers?" he asked, covering both breasts with his hands now, rubbing the flat of his palms lightly across the tips of her nipples. "Or tongue." And with that he leaned down and pressed a wet kiss just on the inside of her knee, leaving her with a tiny swipe of his tongue as he lifted his mouth.

When the only sound filling the air was her hitched breathing, he slowly drew his hands over her breasts, then down over her belly, letting his thumbs rest just above the juncture of her thighs, where her dress was now bunched. "Which is it that you want dipped inside you first, Misty?"

She opened her mouth, but only a little moan came out.

"Are you wet for me?"

She said nothing, her breathing very ragged.

"Tell me, or I'll have you show me."

"Yes," she said roughly.

"Good. I'm going to make you wetter. Do you have any idea how incredibly hard I am for you right now?"

She shook her head.

"I didn't hear you."

"No."

"Would you like to see?"

She trembled hard, then shifted her gaze to his.

"Do you want me to show you exactly what knowing how wet I'm going to make you does to me?"

She jerked her chin in the barest of nods.

"Tell me what you want to see, Misty." He leaned down and braced his hands on the back of the chair, bringing his face close to hers. "I need you to tell me what you want. Everything. Every." He leaned closer. "Last." He ran his tongue along her lower lip. "Thing."

"Take off your clothes," she choked out, her voice rough with need, her accent loose, ragged.

He straightened, stood in front of her, letting his hands drop to his belt. "Why?"

She squirmed in her seat. "I want to see you."

He tugged his shirt free. "Why?" She licked her lips and he twitched hard inside his pants.

She looked at him, there, and he grew even harder. Then she glanced up, desire rolling off of her in waves he swore he could feel. "I need to see."

He ripped his shirt off, making her gasp at the

barely restrained violence of the act. "Need to see what, Misty?" He stepped closer, almost between her legs, so she was forced to look up.

She tipped her head, looked at him, then looked back down, to what was right in front of her face. "All of you."

Staying where he was, discovering his hands were a bit shaky, too, he slowly pulled his belt free, let it drop to the floor. "Do you like what you do to me?"

She nodded, shifting impatiently as he fingered the button of his pants.

"If I freed your hands, what would you do?"

She looked up at him. "Free you."

He grinned down at her as he popped the button, then slowly tugged the zipper down. Then he left them like that and shifted back.

"No!" she said, before she could clamp her lips shut.

"Oh, we'll get there." He reached for the bag again, pulled out the blue strand of beads, and knelt between her legs. "But first, I believe there's some paying back I have to do."

Her eyes widened a bit as he slipped the beads into a glittery pool in one palm, then poured them into the other. Sitting back on his heels, he caught her gaze and held it. "Open for me."

Slowly, she edged her knees apart.

He draped the beads over one bare thigh, then dragged them slowly over her skin, then over the other thigh.

She gasped and twitched hard in her seat.

"How still can you sit?" he asked, drawing the beads along her thighs again.

"Can't," she ground out.

"Can," he ordered. Then he bent his head and kissed the inside of her thigh…before slowly moving upward. He kept his palms flat on the top of her thighs, rolling the beads along one of them as his tongue continued to slide upward on the other. "How wet are you for me now?"

"Very," she growled.

He chuckled, vibrating the heated skin of her inner thigh as he nudged her bunched-up dress higher. "I'm not done yet."

Her hips bucked off the chair when his tongue first brushed against her damp curls. He lifted his head. "Be still. Very still."

She only growled.

He smiled, then speared his tongue inside her, drawing a scream from her as he clamped down on her thighs, preventing her from bucking against him. Again and again, he moved his tongue inside her, groaning himself before finally pulling away. "Very wet indeed," he said, smiling up at her.

But her head was tipped back, her throat working convulsively.

"Watch me," he commanded, waiting for her to straighten, look down.

Her eyes were electric now, desire a live thing glowing inside them. Keeping his gaze locked on that electric glow, he slid the beads slowly up her inner thigh, following the damp path his tongue had just taken.

He watched her eyes widen, then darken almost fiercely as he pushed the beads along the slick crease between her legs. "Wider," he murmured, and, trembling hard now, she fought to relax her knees.

He fought not to untie her and throw her to the floor and take her right then and there.

He wasn't sure who groaned first when he pushed the first bead inside her with his finger. The deep, gutteral sound vibrated from her as he pushed another, and then another. Her hips writhed against the weight of his forearms pressing her down to the chair.

"Look at me," he hoarsely commanded.

She opened eyes that had been squeezed shut as he pushed another bead inside her.

"I want you to hold them inside you as tightly as you hold me."

Her skin was so damp, so perfect, it radiated translucence.

"Hold them," he said again, watching her thighs shake as she willed her muscles to bear down on them.

Then, so slowly he swore he felt them himself, he popped one bead free, pulling up slightly so it tapped against her. Then he tugged again, another bead slipped out. When the third one popped she began to jerk violently as a climax ripped through her so suddenly it took them both by surprise.

And that was his breaking point. He couldn't stand it, couldn't stand that something other than him was touching her, wrenching that kind of pleasure from her. He pushed between her legs, replacing the last bead with his tongue as he continued to drive her so far beyond the edge that she was screaming at him, begging him, for what, neither of them knew, except they didn't want it to ever end.

And when she was done, finally, when she was shuddering, moaning, gasping for breath in the pulse-thickened air, he pushed away, falling back over his own heels, stunned by what they'd done together...and needing her more than he needed his next breath.

And then he was crawling to her, all but ripping the cords from her ankles. He stood, shoving his pants down and off, violently kicking them across the room before shakily grabbing her hips and pulling her straight up from the chair, her wrists still bound behind her. He spun them around, so that he sat in the chair, then yanked her down astride his lap, plunging deep into her with one thrust.

"Yes!" she screamed. So did he.

They fought to join themselves as deeply as they could. And they both shouted all the way up and through first her climax, then his.

And it still wasn't enough. He tore the cord from her wrists so she could bury her hands in his hair, grip his head, pull his face to her breasts and hold on as they continued to ride and thrust. It wasn't enough, he needed more. Deeper. All of her. Claiming.

"Wrap your legs around me." He rose as she complied then turned so they both fell on the bed and he buried himself in her again, still ragingly hard despite how hard he'd come. "Dear God, I'll never have enough of you," he said roughly as he pushed her up the bed with the force of his thrusts. "Never."

"Yes." She held on, rocked up against him, clawing at his back, his hair, his buttocks. "Don't stop."

"No," he said, taking and then taking some more. *Never.* And when she went over again, he was watching her, wanting her all over again just because she stunned him with how beautifully she came apart for him, even as his body finally gave out.

When he slipped out of her and they rolled to their sides, he wouldn't let her go, tangling her body with his, holding on like it was for dear life. And maybe it was. She was dearer to him than anything, any job, any location, anything. He wanted life, with her. He finally found his voice only to discover it was shaky...and with more than exhaustion. "Misty—"

She looked up at him then, a smile of something close to awe curving her lips. "We scare me."

He knew exactly how she felt. But there was something greater than what they'd just done that was even more terrifying. In a wonderful, amazing, fantastic sort of way. It was all but bursting from him, but to give voice to it now...would she think it was the sex talking? "I'm afraid to ask what your other fantasies are," he said, debating, dying.

"I'm afraid to tell you," she said, laughing even as she fought to control her breathing.

He rolled to his back then, pulling her on top of him, suddenly as serious as he'd ever been. "I'm afraid to tell you something, that you'll think it's because of this, that you'll think it's ridiculous, because we just met, that—"

She pushed her hands into his hair, scooted up to kiss him soundly on the mouth. "I just let you tie me to a chair and you're worried that I'm going to think anything you say or do is ridiculous?'' She grinned. ''Please, have a little faith.'' Then she dropped the sweetest kiss to the center of his chest and he just said it. He couldn't help it.

''I love you.''

She stilled, and for a godawful second he thought he'd blown it. Then she looked up at him, her eyes shining with tears and…everything he'd ever wanted to see. ''Thank God,'' she whispered. ''I was worried I was the only one.''

If a person could die from too much happiness, then Tucker suspected he was as good as dead. He rolled her gently to her back, pushed his hand into her hair, framed her face. ''It's not about the sex.''

She burst out laughing even as the first tear escaped the corner of her eye.

He grinned, feeling his own eyes get a bit glassy. ''Okay, so the sex is so-so. We'll work on it.'' She swatted at him and he laughed. ''Misty, you have no idea how much I—'' He was cut off by the ringing of the phone.

They both stilled, looked at each other, as it rang again.

''I don't give a damn who's calling, I'm not answering.''

The ringing stopped and he started to go on with what he'd been saying, when it began ringing again.

He rolled to his back, reached for the receiver and snatched it up. ''Not interested.''

''Tucker? It's Mig.''

He groaned.

"You okay, man? You sick?"

"Hardly."

"Oh." There was a pause, then, "Oh!" in a more knowing tone. "Hey, I'm sorry, man, but the stuff got here early. We want to set it up tonight."

"When tonight?"

"Uh, now?"

Misty rolled on top of him and mouthed, "Go," then kissed his chest again. He was really starting to love that particular little habit of hers.

He swore silently, though, torn.

"Do it," she mouthed, then nipped at him, making him jump.

He locked gazes with hers, promising revenge. She just smiled. "Yeah, okay," he said finally. *You're mine,* he mouthed to her. Then to Mig, he said, "Give me twenty." He hung up without waiting for an answer.

"Fine way to talk to your new partner," she said with that saucy uppercrust smile.

"He's not my partner. And we need to talk about that, too."

She frowned slightly. "Okay. Why don't you come to my hotel when you're done?"

Tucker sat on the edge of the bed. "It will be in the middle of the night, most likely. Maybe not until morning."

Misty crawled up behind him, kissed the side of his neck, then bit his earlobe. "I don't care what time it is."

"You know, we should call Ripley's or something."

"What? Why?"

He turned, then made her squeal by pulling her across his lap. "Because, believe it or not, no matter how many times I have you, I swear whenever you touch me...I want you all over again."

She wiggled her eyebrows...and her hips. "Is that so?"

He laughed and nodded.

"Twenty minutes you say?" she asked, speculatively.

"I can push it to thirty."

"Race you to the shower?"

He grinned. "You're on."

14

MISTY WATCHED HIM SLEEP. It was nine o'clock in the morning. He'd called four hours earlier, as she'd made him promise he would before leaving yesterday. He'd told her he didn't want to bother her, that he'd just head back to his own room to catch up on some sleep. She'd met him there. Softly stroking his cheek, she was very glad she had. When he'd come into the lobby and found her waiting there, a wonderful, surprised smile lit up an exhausted face and tired eyes. And had made the early-morning trip over more than worthwhile.

He'd pulled her against him in the elevator, held her there all the way up to his floor, all the way to the room, where he'd literally dragged her into bed, kissed her, told her he intended to make wild, passionate love to her...then had promptly fallen asleep before he could follow through. Misty hadn't minded in the least. He'd curled his body around hers as if they'd done so every night for years, and slept so soundly she had to watch his chest rise and fall to make sure he was alive.

She pressed a kiss to his heart now. "I want you to get used to coming home to me," she murmured, thinking how much she wanted to be the one there for him at the end of his day, no matter what hour that was.

And with that in mind, she slipped from his bed—their bed—showered and dressed, thankful now she'd thought to bring a change of clothes. She didn't want to waste the time it would take to head back to her hotel to dress. She was excited about the plans she had put into motion yesterday, couldn't wait to tell him later today.

She closed the door quietly behind her, punched the button for the elevator, thinking back on the conversation she'd had with her editor yesterday. Rachel had been very enthusiastic about Misty's new erotic suspense venture. She had to remember to thank Tucker for his very marketable characterization of her story idea. Rachel's enthusiasm was exactly the support she'd needed to see the rest of her plan through. Feeling confident and happier than she could ever remember, she climbed into the taxi. "Sunset Realty, please."

FOUR HOURS and one bid later, Misty let herself back into her hotel room. She was flying high, still amazed at what she'd done. But the little house was perfect. Not right in town, but close enough to sustain the vibe the city had spurred to life inside her. It was entirely different than New York City, which she loved, but she was ready for this change. More than ready. New York would always be there for her, like the steady friend it had always been to her. But new adventures beckoned. She thought she'd be more unsettled about making such a huge decision, such a huge change, yet she felt nothing but the exhilaration and anticipation of getting on with this new phase in her life.

Of course, the neighborhood she'd ended up falling in love with probably wasn't anything like Canyon Springs, but there had been other families there judging by the scatter of bikes, basketball hoops and skateboards she'd seen. She had no idea if she'd be joining them in raising her children there, but it was great knowing she could. They could. Of course, that was providing Tucker didn't completely freak when she told him what she'd done.

Not that they had to move in together. Not right away, anyway, she thought with a private smile. He could get his own place in the city, get started with his new job. They could date.

That made her laugh. She and Tucker…well, they'd skipped right past the dating stage hadn't they?

Now, all she had to do was pray her bid was accepted. And pray Tucker was as excited by her decision as she was. This was all moving so fast, if she let herself think about it too much, she'd be overwhelmed. But it felt right. Just like what was happening between her and Tucker. Jumping in with both feet…not to mention hands, mouths…well, it had worked out pretty bloody well so far. Maybe where love was concerned, there were no rules.

Love. What an immense, fantastic thing.

For perhaps the hundredth time today, she relived the moment he'd told her he loved her. It gave her a hot thrill every time. And she'd never gotten the chance to say the words to him…but she could take care of that right now.

She slipped her purse and the file folder of papers she'd collected from the agent onto the table by the door. The bed was empty, but his clothes were still where they'd landed when he'd peeled out of them at four this morning.

The desk chair was still in the middle of the floor.

Rather than be embarrassed, thinking about what they'd done in that chair, what she'd allowed him to do to her, it aroused her all over again. Which was why she'd left it there after he'd gone yesterday, so she could look at it while she'd stayed in their bed and worked…and remembered everything he made her feel. What they did together would never see the printed page…but there was no denying that the things he'd shown her, taught her about herself, would—should—influence her work. She'd become a Misty Fortune heroine in truth instead of only in fiction.

"Well, they say write what you know," she murmured, a wicked smile curving her lips as she walked over to the chair and ran her hand along the back of it. She shuddered in renewed arousal, hoping he didn't mind continuing their little exploration of her fantasies. And his. For as long as they both wanted to.

With that thought in mind, she slipped out of her clothes, and still smiling, scooped up the other two strands of beads where they'd fallen from the bag to the floor. She slipped them over her head, then plucked two of the silk cords from the floor…and headed to the bathroom where she heard the shower running.

Steam billowed as she stepped into the tiled room. He didn't hear her come in, so she didn't say anything right away, content to watch him through the glass door as he stood beneath the hot spray, running soap over his body. But within minutes she was already dying to touch him, to be the one running her hands over that slick muscled body. So she clicked open the door and slipped in behind him.

He didn't startle when she slid her hands down his back, then around his waist, pressing herself up against him. A little moan slipped out of its own volition at the contact. She didn't think she'd ever have enough of him.

"Hi," he said, his voice still rough with sleep.

"You knew I was here."

"As it turns out, I like being watched." He turned, his slick skin all slippery and warm as it rubbed over hers. "By you." He took her mouth without even opening his eyes, pushed his fingers through her hair and stepped back, taking her with him, so the water streamed over both of them. His kiss went on...and on, until she could barely stand upright, her need for him so strong.

Without speaking, he pulled the beads off and let them fall to the shower floor. The silk cords followed a moment later when he grabbed her hips and lifted her from her feet. He backed her against the tile, thrusting inside of her even as she wrapped her legs around his waist and grabbed his head to pull his mouth back to hers. They growled and groaned, panted and gasped, then growled some more as he continued pushing himself inside of her.

Her orgasm was like a hot whip of pleasure, lashing at her repeatedly, wrenching one sobbing moan after another from somewhere deep inside her. Tucker buried his face in the curve of her neck, water beating on his back as he grunted his way through his own climax, pushing, pulsing, pushing some more, until they both collapsed breathlessly against the wet tile.

It was long minutes later, when their bodies stopped shuddering, their breathing became less labored, that he finally lifted his head and dropped a heartbreakingly sweet kiss on her lips. "Hi."

She smiled. "Remind me to always start my day in the shower with you."

He let her feet slide to the floor, then slid his hands up her arms and into her hair, pulling her to him for a longer, more drugging kiss. "I think we can work that out." He tasted her mouth again, then her chin, then her jaw and her ear, then her mouth again. "You're like this addiction. I can't get enough of you."

She kissed him, smiled. "I know exactly what you mean." She held his gaze. "I love you, Tucker."

His eyes went darker and hotter, if that was possible. His hands tightened almost painfully on her shoulders as he continued to stare into her eyes, speechless. "Again," he finally managed. "Say it."

She slipped her arms around his waist, kissed his chin, his cheek, the corner of his eyes, which closed as a hiss of pleasure streamed through his lips. "I love you," she whispered against his ear.

She rested her cheek on his shoulder, let him pull her tightly into his arms. She felt his heart thunder beneath his chest, almost harder than when he'd been buried deep inside her.

"It's...insane," he said hoarsely, "how impossibly

fantastic that makes me feel. How you make me feel. Insane." He tipped her head back, looked into her eyes. "But it's even better to be able to say it back to you. I love you, Amethyst Fortuna Smythe-Davies." He kissed her smiling, was grinning even more widely when he lifted his head. "I want to whoop and holler, I want to open the windows and shout it to the world. How wild is that?"

"Pretty wild," she said, her heart expanding with so much feeling she thought it would burst. "Beautifully, wonderfully, wild." She kissed his heart. "And I'm happy to hear it, because I have something else to tell you, about where I've been this morning."

"Did you talk to your editor yesterday?"

"As a matter of fact, I did, but that's not—"

"What did she say? Did she go for your new idea?"

"As a matter of fact, she loved the idea."

He hugged her, turned them both around and let the water spray them both in the face, making them splutter even as he kissed her.

She was laughing as she ducked back out of the spray. "Have I mentioned that I enjoy your enthusiasm about my work?"

"I could say the same to you."

"Good, because I've been dying to ask you how it all went last night. Any additional clues? Did the laser analysis reveal anything new?"

As if it were the most natural thing in the world, and with him, she thought perhaps everything would, he turned her so her back was to him, then tipped her head back so he could massage shampoo into her hair as he talked. She could have told him she'd already washed her hair this morning, but she was too busy groaning. "Your hands are pure magic."

He stepped in closer and slid them down her back to cup her buttocks. "So I've been told."

She wiggled her backside. "Pretty cheeky, ducks."

He laughed, then pushed her head under the spray to rinse the suds, kissing her quiet when she spluttered.

When they came up for air, he went on with the conversation as if nothing had happened. She loved that about him, too. Playful, unpredictable, dedicated. Hers.

"Well, a couple of things happened. They pulled the taxi driver in but he couldn't positively ID Ralston in a lineup. He thought the guy he saw might have been shorter. Ralston willingly underwent a polygraph, which did back up his assertion that he wasn't involved, not that a lie detector test is one hundred percent reliable, but the case against him is getting shakier all the time. The laser analysis was interesting, fascinating really, but not as forthcoming as we'd hoped. Except it did indicate that the shooter was likely shorter than Ralston, or had shorter arms anyway."

"Like a woman's arms maybe?" Misty asked, fascinated by the whole process. "Any luck finding the girlfriend?"

Tucker shut the water off and pulled two heated towels into the shower, wrapping one around her body, the other around her hair.

"You know," she said on an appreciative sigh, "for someone who escaped the suffocating pampered lifestyle of her youth and embraced her absolute independence—" she lifted onto her toes and kissed him hard on the mouth "—I'm discovering there is something to be said about being pampered after all."

Tucker merely bowed and opened the shower door for her.

"What about your towel?" she asked.

He stepped out behind her, then pulled her back against him, rubbing her towel-clad body over him with such enthusiasm, she giggled, making her towel turban collapse.

"There," he announced, setting her away from him. "All dry."

She'd never tire of him. "God, I don't think I've ever laughed so much in my life."

"Great, isn't it?" He tugged her back against him when she turned toward the counter for her comb. He kissed the side of her neck, then behind her ear. "I want you all the time," he said a bit breathlessly.

"It's honestly amazing, isn't it?" she responded, knowing exactly how he felt.

"Honestly," he agreed, kissing along her neck, down to her shoulder. "Amazing."

Laughing again, she swatted him away and moved from his arms. "Let me pull a comb through this mess before it's a rat's nest. And you can tell me about the girlfriend."

Tucker took the comb from her hand and began working on the curls in the back as he stood behind her. "As far as we can tell, there really isn't one."

Misty tipped her head back as he pulled the comb in long smooth strokes through her hair. Could nothing this man do to her not feel like heaven? "So, no other clues about the other lipstick?'' she asked between sighs of contentment.

''Not yet. It doesn't match any of the shades Denton had at the house either.''

''Hmm,'' Misty said, wheels beginning to turn as Tucker continued his incredibly relaxing ministrations. ''What if…'' She trailed off, letting her thoughts continue to spin out, until a theory rose from the swirl. She turned, plucking the comb from his fingers and laying it on the counter, her thoughts exclusively on the case.

Tucker grinned so widely, she paused. ''What?''

''You get this almost fierce look of determination when the creative brain kicks in, then you just light up when things click into place.''

She gave him a mock arch look. ''I'm so glad I can amuse you.''

He shrugged, unrepentant. ''I love watching you work.''

She smiled. ''Good, because I think I may have a lead for you.''

He folded his arms and leaned against the counter, wholly unconcerned with his state of undress. She rather liked that about him.

''Oh you do, do you?''

She swallowed a snicker, knowing he couldn't have realized her thoughts. ''I was just thinking, all along we've assumed it was Ralston's girlfriend because of the lipstick on the jacket. But you say the shooter has shorter arms than Ralston. And the cabbie says the guy who got out at the gate was maybe shorter. So, what if it wasn't him wearing the jacket…but her?''

"I don't follow."

"Well, maybe Ralston's telling the truth and he wasn't there that night. All we know is that his jacket definitely was. So was the lipstick. Which means the wearer of the lipstick was there, probably wearing his jacket. A jacket he swears he left in his club. So what woman has access to his club, knows his routine?"

"We've been down that path. His assistant fits that profile, but she's been questioned at length, as have others who know them both, and we can't link them together. And yes, they got a warrant, but no match on her lipsticks either."

"Did you check her purse? If she was wearing it that night, it was likely she had it with her."

"Yes."

"Damn." She chewed her bottom lip. "Okay. There's something else that's been bugging me about all this. Why would the girlfriend kill her lover's wife, presumably to clear the way for them to be together, then plant the jacket at his place, framing him for the crime?" Her eyes went wide as the sudden realization hit her. She snapped her fingers, then pointed at Tucker. "Unless!"

He grabbed her finger, and grinning, pulled her to him. "Unless what?"

"Did anyone test the lipstick on Ms. Denton?"

Tucker frowned. "You mean the lipstick she used. Yes, it didn't match."

She smiled slyly up at him. "No, I mean the lipstick on her actual lips. What I'm wondering is, is there more than one shade of lipstick on Patsy Denton's lips?"

"Meaning—"

"Meaning it wasn't Ralston's girlfriend, but Patsy Denton's." She mockingly blew on her fingernails and buffed them on her towel. "Crime of passion after all. Only Patsy Denton's jealous lover was a woman."

Tucker just shook his head. "Incredible."

"But possible."

"Oh, I'm not saying it's not. Not at all. In fact, it makes perfect, if twisted sense."

"You know what they say, truth is stranger than fiction. And if anyone can vouch for that, I can."

He dropped a fast kiss on her mouth, then headed to the bedroom.

"Where are you going?"

"To put a call in to Mig and Henderson, tell them to reinterview Patsy Denton's employees, dig a little deeper into her personal life. You hungry?"

She stopped in the bathroom doorway. "Again?"

He paused in the middle of dialing and shot her a very wicked grin. "Why, Ms. Smythe-Davies, how very naughty of you."

She gave a little curtsy. "I try. But honestly, Tucker, you'll never make a decent Brit."

He simply smiled and finished his call to Mig, then put in another to room service and ordered a startling amount of food.

"I can see one of us has an appetite," she said, heading to the closet.

He surprised her by literally leaping across the bed and snatching her off her feet, making her squeal. They both landed in the middle of the unmade bed, with Misty sprawled on top.

Her towel had come off at some point, and their damp skin clung to each other. As usual with him, she was once again breathless and laughing. "What was that for?"

"Mig told me to thank you for your insights. He thinks you pegged it."

"And he suggested tackling me to the bed as his way of showing appreciation?"

"Oh no, that was because you mocked my hunger." He kissed her fast and deep, until she was gasping for more than air. "So I thought maybe you needed a demonstration about why I have to eat like a horse to maintain my energy levels."

She laughed, then batted her eyelashes and tried her best Southern drawl. "Why, I'd much rather discuss another element of your...personality that has equine-like comparisons."

Tucker burst out laughing as he rolled her beneath them. "Okay, okay, I surrender."

She batted her eyelashes again, though it was hard not to laugh. "Why, whatever do you mean, suh?"

"I promise to leave the Brit accent to you, if you promise to leave the Southern belle routine to the Southern belles."

She widened her eyes in mock offense, then tugged her hand up between them, stuck it out, and very calmly said, "Deal."

Tucker eyed her closely. "I've been had." She simply batted her lashes at him again. Smiling, he took her hand, turned it palm out, dropped a hot kiss there, then pulled one of her fingers into his mouth, making her gasp.

He let it slide out slowly. "Deal."

"Well," she said, taking a moment to let her heart get back to normal. "Remind me to seal deals with you more often. And speaking of deals, there's something we need to talk about."

He looked at her. "Sounds serious."

"It is."

Frowning a little, he scooted them both up, then rolled to his side, propping up on one elbow. "Good serious or bad serious?"

She liked it that he automatically assumed it was something they were going to deal with together. "Good, I hope. It's about where I went this morning, while you were sleeping. About some non-fiction research I needed to do, only I ended up doing a bit more than just research. After I called the airlines, I—"

"Wait," he broke in. "I need to say something first. I know you're supposed to leave tomorrow, head back to New York."

"But that's why I called them, I—" He stopped her with a finger pressed across her lips.

"I called the airlines today, too."

That surprised her so much she stopped trying to finish. "You did? Why?"

"I don't want to—can't—have a long-distance relationship with you. Hell, I can barely stand you being gone for a couple of hours while I'm sleeping, and you were still in the same city, for Christ's sake." He laughed and shook his head. "And I'm not even the possessive type."

She grinned and traced a finger over his lower lip. "Well, I am, I'll have you know. Which is why—"

He kissed her fingertip, then talked over her. "I turned down the job here."

"I cancelled my reservations and made an appointment with a—" She stopped as his words registered. "You what? What did you just say?"

"You cancelled your flight?"

She nodded. "But you first. What did you do? Why did you turn them down?" She had a sudden fleeting sense of panic.

"I booked myself on your flight." He let out a brief, disbelieving laugh. "The one you're no longer on."

"You did?" He'd planned to come back to New York with her? Then she put it together. "Oh no."

He framed her face, slicked her wet hair back, then ran his thumbs over her cheeks. "Oh yes. I wanted to surprise you. I already put a call in to New York. Mig gave me some names. I'm going to check into one of the forensic teams they have there, see what I can come up with." He searched her face. "Don't worry. I want to do this. I want to be where you are, but this doesn't mean I'm—"

He stopped when she started to laugh.

"What? What's wrong?"

"Nothing," she said, then kissed him soundly. "Nothing at all. While you were arranging to come be part of my world, I was arranging to be part of yours."

"What do you mean?"

"My non-fiction research this morning. It was for a house. Here. For me. One I hoped would eventually be our home."

"You went house hunting?" He looked awestruck.

She nodded.

"Without me?" He stuck out his bottom lip.

Now it was her turn to be surprised. Then she laughed and shook her head. "And here I was afraid you'd get nervous, that I was moving too fast. But I didn't want to be where you weren't. I figured you'd probably want your own place in the city." She stroked her fingers into his hair and gave him a sly smile. "Then I'd hoped to lure you into our new home slowly, move your things in a little at a time, until you just ended up there with me full-time."

He grinned now. "How very calculating of you."

"Plotting is what I do for a living, after all." She turned more serious. "You like it here, right? I know I do. And it's closer to your old friends. Is it too late to take Mig's offer? We can go look at other houses if you want. I haven't signed anything yet. Or we can live here in the city together, I don't care. I just knew family was important to you and—"

He kissed her into silence. When he finally lifted his head, his expression was filled with wonder...and desire. "I love you. I want us to be together, here, New York, I don't care. I want you to have what you need, too. All the rest can happen when it's right. We'll figure it out as we go."

"That's worked pretty well so far."

"I think so."

"So," she asked, "can we stay in Vegas?"

"Is that truly what you want?"

She nodded. "I like the vibe here, the energy. It's so different from New York."

"What about your publisher? Won't they be upset?"

"As long as I have a computer, a printer and a post office, I can work anywhere."

"That's convenient," he said, then began dropping light kisses all over her face.

"What about you?" she asked, smiling through his rain of kisses. "Are you sure you want to leave Canyon Springs?"

"Yes," he said, kissing her on the mouth. "What I want isn't a place. It's you, it's loving what I do, building a life around those things."

"You know, I've spent a good deal of time cutting myself off from things, clinging to being independent," she said. "I never thought about family." She smiled wryly. "Other than to be glad I was no longer under the influence of mine."

He started to speak, but she stopped him with a finger laid across his lips.

"But when we were driving through the neighborhoods today, I was looking for a place for you, that you'd want to raise children in. And it slowly occurred to me that I wanted it, too. Really wanted it. It's quite terrifying actually, because I never had a home, not the kind you had. But I want it." She looked directly into his eyes. "At some point. With you."

"Well, you're a pretty fast learner." He grinned. "I think I could help you out. Show you the familial ropes, as it were."

"I'm counting on it," she said, then hugged him tightly, overcome by what life had handed her so suddenly. "My partner in fantasy exploration." She smiled then, tears burning in her eyes, tears of sheer, unadulterated joy. "And perhaps that was my most forbidden fantasy of all. Love, family, home."

"We'll have it all, Misty. After all, a writer deserves her happily-ever-after, doesn't she?"

There was a knock on the door. "Room service."

"But first," he said, a wicked gleam entering his dark, beautiful eyes. "Have you ever had any food sex fantasies? Because I have some strawberries and cream I'd like to interest you in."

She rolled to her back as he got up, grabbed her damp towel and wrapped it around his hips as he strode to the door. So confident, so beautiful. So hers.

"As it happens, I love strawberries. What do you plan to do with them?"

He took care of the waiter, closed the door and rolled the heavily laden cart to the center of the room himself. Steam rose from several covered dishes. He took the covers off, then slipped the linen napkin from the tray and walked over to where she'd perched on the edge of the bed. Without saying a word he tied it around her eyes.

"You'll see," he said, and she could hear the wicked promise in his voice.

She shivered in anticipation. Of what he'd do to her now, and what he'd be doing to her, with her, in all the years to come. "I can't wait."

They're strong, they're sexy, they're not afraid to use the assets Mother Nature gave them....

Venus Messina is...

#916 **WICKED & WILLING**
by Leslie Kelly
February 2003

Sydney Colburn is...

#920 **BRAZEN & BURNING**
by Julie Elizabeth Leto
March 2003

Nicole Bennett is...

#924 **RED-HOT & RECKLESS**
by Tori Carrington
April 2003

The Bad Girls Club...where membership has its privileges!

Available wherever

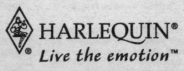

is sold....

HARLEQUIN®
Live the emotion™

Visit us at www.eHarlequin.com

HTBGIRLS

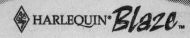